PALE HORSE

Book Description

Follow our ragtag gang as they endure the trials of the fourth seal in this upbeat and lighthearted adventure story. Zombies, alien moss, and a trip to Mars included.

(Book 4) Our ragtag characters must endure the opening of the fourth seal and the violence, famine, pestilence, and beasts that it brings. The zombies have returned, the alien moss has morphed into something more destructive, and The Community has begun taking the tainted biological warfare vaccine again. Will they be able to escape from Death and the aliens? Or will they finally reach their breaking point and be fed to the bioship? Find out by tagging along with the gang in this lighthearted and upbeat story.

This is the fourth book in the seven-book Seven Seals Redux series.

PALE HORSE

Seven Seals Redux, #4

Connie Myres

ConnieMyres.com
FEATHER AND FERMION PUBLISHING

FEATHER AND FERMION PUBLISHING - MICHIGAN

*Dedicated to my family and friends, especially my sons
Lucas and Charles Kraus for their loyal support
and encouragement of all my projects.
I appreciate you.*

Table of Contents

ONE

Revelation 6: 7– 8. 7 When he opened the fourth seal, I heard the voice of the fourth living creature say, "Come!" 8 And I saw, and behold, a pale horse, and its rider's name was Death, and Hades followed him; and they were given power over a fourth of the earth, to kill with sword and with famine and with pestilence and by wild beasts of the earth.

* * *

"All hell's breaking loose," Max said, stepping into the guard tower situated next to the entrance of the prepper compound. "People are getting cranky because we're on a forced starvation diet and the return of the zombies is getting on everyone's nerves, including mine." He moved next to Jack, Tony, and Ray, looking out the open windows covered with camouflage netting. "Have you seen any more of those bastard zombies?"

Ray looked at Max; watching him adjust his thick-lensed glasses as if they were binoculars. "There's a couple out there, wandering around like lost sheep."

"You haven't experienced being chased by those damned things. Lost sheep isn't how I'd describe them," Jack said, looking out over the alien moss covered Michigan forest outside the compound walls. "I think a better description would be Hunters from Hell."

"I agree with Jack," Max said, placing his bony elbows on a windowsill. "You astronauts are too nice. You'll need to be a little more cynical if you want to hang out with us."

"Who else am I going to hang out with? Out there with those things?" Ray said, adjusting the M16 slung over his shoulder. Tony had gotten it from the preppers and given it to him when they landed outside the compound in the Pegasus space capsule. He wanted their group of survivors armed.

"There's one of those Hunters from Hell right now," Tony said, pointing past the motorhome and Max's white Mustang, toward the dying pine forest and the road leading from the prepper fortress.

A man, with shoulders hunched and arms dangling, meandered, as if confused and unable to find what it was searching for. It slipped and stumbled on the slimy residue left from the pink moss as the plant digested all the vegetation it attached itself to.

"I thought those zombies died," Max said, leaning forward on the open window's sill to examine the dying body as it stumbled around. "Must be they all didn't turn into cocoons and hatch those creatures that pull themselves over the ground with those damned gangling arms of theirs."

"They're called tornens," Tony said, keeping his eye to the riflescope while he watched the zombie look left and right, never seeming to focus on anything.

"Remember? That's what you said those aliens on the spaceship called them, and it sounded like they were good to eat."

"That's right; they said it was a delicacy. I think they ate it just before it hatched out of the zombies' guts," Jack said, taking the alien pistol from the back waistband of his jeans. The aliens had taken his Kimber pistol, but this alien gun was superior. He and Tony had practiced with it when they had gotten back to the compound a few weeks ago. They found it had some type of auto-aim feature, had strength settings, including stun, and even recharged itself. However, Jack remembered while they were outside the creature corral on Mars, that the human workers, and likely the aliens, were able to block it and render it useless.

"Before it hatches, its flesh is probably less tough," Max said, shaking his head. "Still had to be ugly, though."

"I'm so hungry I'd eat one," Jack said, rubbing his stomach in jest.

Max lowered his eyebrows and looked at Jack. "You go right ahead and do that, Jack."

"There's another zombie out there," Tony said, still looking through his scope.

"How are they finding us?" Ray asked. "We're deep in the woods; you wouldn't think there'd be a lot of people around here."

"I think they can smell us," Jack said.

"I wouldn't think their decaying bodies would have a working olfactory system, but who knows," Max said, sniffing.

"The aliens are sending them our way," Tony said, keeping an eye to the sight as he raised it above the treetops.

"I'm surprised you didn't say it was the Men in Black doing it," Max scoffed.

"It's the spores," Jack said. "It's like that zombie ant spore that somehow guides the ant to where it needs to go. I can't remember what the professor called it."

"You have your thinking cap on again today, Jack," Max said, not impressed. "The zombie ant spore is called Ophiocordyceps unilateralis, but I don't know what type of spore the aliens are using. The fungus growing inside the zombies seems to guide them to places that are dark and humid . . . so that that damned tornen thing can grow inside them."

"They should be done with all that," Jack said, moving his shoulder length hair behind an ear. It had grown out from the time he, Max, Father, and Tony had shaved their heads and faces when they were trapped inside the Walmart store salon. Now they looked like hippies.

"That's right, it hatches in a matter of days, not weeks," Max said, cocking his head toward Jack. "It's funny we're talking about zombies like we're hunting white-tailed deer."

Jack laughed. "So why are these things still walking around?"

Max shrugged. "I don't know."

"Have you seen any of those hatched tornens out there?" Ray asked, perking up.

"Not yet," Tony said. "But I'm lookin'."

"At least the compound is pretty secure," Ray said, looking at the perimeter fence. "Good thing the preppers thought ahead."

Tony lowered his scope and looked at the fortified community. "They call themselves members of The

Community, not preppers. But yeah, the compound is surrounded on three sides by an eight-foot high precast concrete fence. The front gate is made of steel tubing, but there's no fence on the lakeside . . . hopefully, zombies can't swim."

"Right now they seem pretty damned dumb," Max said. "But I'd keep an eye on them. I wouldn't be surprised if their mush brains have the ability to think and learn."

"Don't worry," Tony said. "I plan on spending most of my time up here monitoring the perimeter. In fact, I think we should all take turns in the guard tower so that it's manned twenty-four-seven."

Then a couple people could be heard arguing from the compound courtyard.

"I did not take the bread, Clarice," a man dressed in dark clothes and a broad-brimmed hat shouted in anger.

"Then who was it?" a woman snapped back. She clenched the apron over her long dress. "You were the only one in the kitchen."

"It was not me," the man shouted with anger.

"I see crumbs on your shirt," the woman said so loudly she was almost screaming.

Everyone in the guard tower, except Tony, who was keeping an eye on the zombies, moved to the opposite window. They looked into the center of the compound where a man and woman were airing their disgust of each other in public.

"The people of The Community are a little unstable," Ray said, watching the spectacle.

"Yep," Max said, shaking his head. "That biological warfare vaccine they were taking, until the professor made them stop, turned some of them into fruitcakes."

"I still can't get over how it made their bones grow and protrude, especially on their faces," Ray said. "It makes their eyes bulge out and their skin sink in like shrink wrap."

"I think we should watch them," Jack said, crossing his arms. "Now that the zombies are back I wouldn't be surprised if they decide to begin taking that vaccine again."

"I agree with Jack," Tony said, still watching the two zombies wandering in the woods. "As far as I'm concerned, the only people we can trust are the people in our group. Not even the Cartwrights, Parkers, or the Hogans."

Jack rubbed the gold coin, still in his jean pocket, between his thumb and forefinger. He felt the portrait of the half-breed alien, Rausuca, on the obverse side, and the hieroglyphics on the reverse. "Yeah, I agree with you. I think they're hiding something. As nice of a guy as their leader Cecil Hogan is . . . there's something he's not telling us."

"Based on what you told me about that room in the church always being locked, and the odd way they say grace," Ray said. "It just isn't normal."

"That room's called the sacristy and they say heavenly brothers instead of Christ in their prayers," Jack said. "These aren't your usual preppers, they're more like a cult."

"Why hasn't anyone asked them about it?" Ray asked, watching the man and woman continue to argue as people began coming out of their homes.

"We don't want to rock the boat and be cast out of the compound. It's safer in here than being out there," Jack said. "That vaccine made them all a little moody."

"It seems to me that when they say, heavenly brothers, they're talking about the aliens," Ray said. "And it's possible that locked room has something inside that might help us."

A loud smack of a hand against skin caught their attention.

"That woman just slapped that guy," Jack said. He chuckled as he watched her run back inside her house.

They watched as the man stood alone in the courtyard. He put his hands on his hips and shouted, "Cecil Hogan, get out here."

"Looks like shit's going to hit the fan," Max said, reaching for the pack of cigarettes he used to have in the breast pocket of his work shirt. "Damn it, I could really use a smoke right now."

Moments later Cecil came out of the hospital, where the professor was working in the lab, and approached the man. "What is the problem, Amos?"

"The food is gone and my wife is accusing me of stealing bread. She even sees imaginary breadcrumbs on my shirt," he wiped his mouth with the side of his hand. "We need food. I suggest you send those scavengers to find it. We would still have enough food if they weren't here. You should never have allowed them to stay."

"Oh, shit," Jack said, straightening his posture. "I think we wore out our welcome. They'll be kicking our butts to the curb pretty soon."

"We better do something," Max said, adjusting his glasses.

"I'll go talk to Cecil," Jack said. "Are you guys up to leaving the compound and searching for food out in zombie land."

"Whatever it takes," Tony said. "We do need food and maybe we could find fuel for the space capsule."

Max shook his head. "And where do you propose we find fuel for Pegasus? We're out here in the middle of nowhere." He cupped his unshaven chin with his finger and thumb and then turned to Ray. "What kind of fuel does that thing use? Liquid hydrogen and oxygen?"

"The Pegasus uses methalox, liquid methane, and liquid oxygen," Ray answered. "It uses smaller tanks and is easier to store than hydrogen. It can even be manufactured on Mars. Water and carbon dioxide can be converted to CH4. It's a good choice for deep space missions." He paused and then asked, "Why? Are we going for a ride?"

"If we get kicked out of here, I'm just . . . just looking at our options."

"Well, if taking Pegasus for a ride is in your plans," Ray said, turning to look at the spacecraft sitting outside the compound's main entrance. "I'll need liquid methane; you'll find it in one of those LNG cryogenic tanker transport trailers. I'll take care of getting the oxygen oxidizer ready."

"Cryogenic? How cold does methane need to be?" Max asked, studying the capsule, tarnished from the heat of re-entry.

"The stuff you'll be bringing to me needs to be minus two-hundred-sixty degrees Fahrenheit, that changes it from a gas to a liquid," Ray said. "But if you're planning a deep space mission we'll need another spacecraft because Pegasus isn't designed to go to Mars."

"Where would we find a craft like that?" Jack asked.

"We'd have to go to the Intercosmic Space Program's main base in Wisconsin and use the new deep-space craft they just developed . . . Infinity One."

"Seems like we'd be better off just flying an airplane to get out of here," Jack said, still watching the growing commotion in the center of the compound. "Does anyone know how to fly one?"

Everyone shook their heads except Ray. "I can fly one but using Pegasus is a better option."

"Cattle fart out methane," Tony said, matter-of-factly.

"So what are you saying, Tony," Max said, annoyed. "We're supposed to go around and gather cow manure?"

"I'm just sayin'," Tony said, unflustered by Max's derisive remark.

Max refocused his thoughts. "There are a lot of natural gas wells in this part of Michigan and I think there is a refinery around here, someplace. And I believe methane is the primary ingredient in natural gas. Would that work as fuel for Pegasus?"

"As long as it's liquefied natural gas, LNG, and in a cooled tanker; not the stuff transported in trucks like propane is," Ray said. "It won't be pure methane, but it will be our best shot, especially since we're not near ISP or NASA to get fuel."

Jack saw the man point at them with a face red from anger. "We better do something."

"I'll go with you, Jack, to talk with them," Max said, once again reflexively reaching into his shirt pocket for the long gone pack of cigarettes. "Since I'm staying at Cecil's house, I may get further with them than you."

TWO

Max and Jack walked down the guard tower steps, toward Cecil and the fuming man. They stopped a few feet from them.

"Is there a problem, Cecil?" Max asked, clearing his throat.

Before Cecil could answer, the agitated man said, "Problem? Of course, there's a problem; our food is almost gone. You and your . . greedy group of people have eaten into our reserves, leaving our families to starve."

Max did not know what to say. It was true their group ate their food, but they kept on the rations without complaining. "I'm sorry, but the professor is working on a way to get the most benefit from the seeds we have left, without that moss affecting them."

"The seeds are not your seeds; they are our seeds. You and your people had nothing to do with them. If it weren't for our planning you'd all be dead," the man said, thrusting a fist toward Max as if he was ready to fistfight.

Cecil stepped forward. "Amos, we have received benefit from him and his companions. They returned order to The Community by removing Randy from authority, and Professor Dillon has been helping with his seed experiments."

The man stomped his foot. "Experiments, that's all they are. How do we know they have our best interest at heart? For all we know they could be planning to take over The Community, the greenhouse, and any remaining nourishment."

Jack watched as a crowd of onlookers began forming around them. He saw the professor, Father Mitch, Clare, and Sarah make their way through the gathered people and approach them. "We appreciate the help you've given us but—"

"No buts, no explaining," the man said. He turned to Cecil and then toward the gathering. He raised his voice and said loud enough for everyone to hear, "I say they must leave the compound. We cannot support them. They are leeches. Let's take a vote."

"No vote," Cecil said, raising his hands to get everyone's attention. "I suggest we continue to work together."

A woman from the crowd walked up to Cecil, extending her arm. "Look at my skin. I am coming down with a disease." She pointed to several blisters on her forearm. "And it's not just me, others have it too."

"When did this begin?" Cecil asked, surprised by the new development.

"This morning, we woke up with it," a man said, walking forward, his face covered with serum-filled vesicles. "I think we're turning into zombies. We should never have listened to their professor, and should never have stopped taking the BW vaccine. They had this planned all along."

The professor was out of breath from walking his massive body through the increasing crowd. He had come from the hospital where he had a makeshift lab set up. "That is not true. The BW vaccine was causing serious side effects and it was . . . it is in your best interest to not take it."

The crowd was agitated, becoming noisy. Jack looked at Sarah, who seemed terrified, and then whispered to Max. "You'd better say something before we're flogged."

Max looked at Cecil. "Again, we mean the members of The Community no harm. We'll go find food and bring it back to you." He moved his eyes from Cecil, who was staying silent, and looked at the noisy crowd. Even though his knees were shaking uncontrollably underneath his khaki work pants, he continued, "As you know, I am a scientist. The professor and I have been working diligently to find a solution to the alien invasion and their ability to alter the environment. Don't forget that we have done our best to keep the food supply safe. If you had planted your seeds in the fields with the moss, they would have been lost. If you had irrigated your gardens with the contaminated lake water . . . they would have been lost. We have protected The Community, assisted with repairs, and . . ." Max lost his train of thought when he saw one of Randy's thugs walk into the circle of people with an M16 rifle slung over his shoulder, and then up to Cecil.

"Don't forget they left our beloved Randy stranded on the alien spaceship," the man with the assault rifle said, loud enough for all to hear.

Sarah walked up next to Jack as the crowd became angry and loud. She whispered, "Jack, what got into them? What happened?"

Jack whispered back, "I don't know, other than they're hungry and they're blaming us." He turned to Max. "We'd better appease them before Randy's thugs reclaim The Community and we're either put in jail or forced outside the fence . . . and probably without our weapons."

Max nodded. "A few of us will gather our things, find food, and bring it back here. Is that a deal?"

"No deal," the man with the gun shouted. "All of your gang must leave. When you return with food, then we will talk."

Another one of Randy's cohorts walked up, gripping a rifle. "Some of their gang must stay here because what reason would they have to return with food? I say the women, kids, and dogs stay. They will surely return with food to save them."

"Save them?" Jack spoke up, his eyebrows raised. "What do you mean by that?"

The man smirked, raised his rifle above his head, and shouted, "Cecil Hogan has done us a disfavor by allowing these infidels to stay here and deplete our supplies. So I, Daniel Fisher, am taking control of The Community from Cecil Hogan on behalf of Randy Watson."

Jack took Sarah's hand and began backing away, as some in the crowd cheered, and others stood mute, likely afraid to counter Daniel's self-appointed leadership. He whispered, "They'll probably take our weapons next and I don't want to part with my alien pistol."

"What are you going to do?" Sarah whispered, following his lead.

"Get the kids and Clare, and all of you stay with the Cartwrights. They'll probably keep you the safest of any of them. And hide that magic wand; I'm sure they'll take that, too."

Sarah nodded as Jack released her and backed toward the guard tower where Tony was walking down to meet him.

"What's going on?" Tony asked, gripping his rifle.

"Randy's thugs just took control of the compound. They're keeping the women and kids as hostage while us men are kicked out. I don't want to shoot anyone, but I'm sure they'll be over here to take our weapons next."

Jack watched as Sarah, Clare, and the kids went into the Cartwrights, followed by a third man with an M16. He saw Father Mitch talking with Daniel; that was, until he lowered his gun and pointed it at the old priest. Soon Father Mitch, Max, and the professor were heading their way, followed by two of the gunmen.

The six men stood at the front gate as Daniel and his armed sidekick pointed their guns at them. Max, Father, and the professor had their hands already raised, while Jack, Tony, and Ray stood their ground.

"Hand over your weapons," Daniel demanded.

"We won't be able to get the food and bring it back here if we don't have a way to fight the zombies," Jack said.

"You'll figure out a way," Daniel said, leering at Jack. "We have your women, you'll be back. Hand them over."

"We may be back," Jack said, "but not with food. We can't fight our way to the food and then back here without weapons."

"Okay, then," Daniel said, after thinking a moment. "Tony and Ray can keep their rifles, but the alien gun you have, Jack, stays here."

Jack was not giving up the pistol they had gotten from the alien spaceship; it was too powerful. Before the gunmen had time to react, Jack had the alien gun pulled from his back waistband and had it aimed at Daniel. "This gun stays with us. It's our safe passage to the food and then back here." He looked straight into Daniels bulging eyes. "You do want to eat, don't you?"

The crowd that was gathering around them began to run away while Daniel and Jack glared at each other with itchy fingers on their gun triggers.

"Three days," Daniel said, spitting on the ground. "You have three days to bring us food or the women and children die."

"No, Daniel," Mrs. Cartwright said. She and Cecil had walked up behind him. "We are a people of peace. Why are you doing this?"

While Daniel and Jack kept guns pointed at each other, the other gunman pointed his rifle at Cecil.

Without taking his eyes off Jack, Daniel said, "True, enough. We are a people of peace, but we are also people who have been taken advantage of by these parasites. The time has come for these heathens to pay their due. Both of you know they do not believe in the teachings of The Community. They are only one-step above the walking dead who have now found our compound and will be trying to get inside. Open the gate, John."

When the gate was open, the men stepped out, scanning the area for zombies. They did not see any, but they knew they could not be far away.

"Three days," Daniel said, closing the gate behind them.

THREE

Tony looked up at the guard tower and saw Daniel and John had already run up the steps and were watching them. "The keys had better be in the RV; there's no way we're walking out of here."

They ran to the Class A gas coach and closed the door. The professor sat in his usual recliner while Tony and Jack went to the cab.

"They never took them out," Tony said, seated in the driver's seat. He turned the ignition and the motorhome sprang to life. He swung it around, drove past Max's Mustang, and down the gravel road. "Any idea where we're headed?"

Jack sat in the passenger seat and picked up the map lying on the console. He unfolded it while Ray stood behind the cab seats.

"One place we need is a natural gas refinery so that we can get methane for the spacecraft," Max said, sitting on the couch next to Father.

The professor looked at Max. "Methane for the spacecraft? What do you have in mind?"

Max took his heavy glasses off, cleaned them with his dirty shirttail, and put them back on his greasy nose. "It sounds crazy, but if worse comes to worse, we can leave the compound in Pegasus."

"And go where?" the professor asked, forcing his fatty bottom to fit better in the recliner seat.

"Any place but here," Max said, leaning back. He swung both elbows over the back of the sectional, trying to get relaxed. "But likely Wisconsin."

"What's wrong with driving the motorhome?" Father asked.

Max looked out the window. "See that moss, Father? It's killing all the vegetation . . . covering everything in sight." He looked back at the priest. "Did you see the sores on those people's skin? Earth is becoming unfit to live on. Ray says there's a spaceship designed for deep space missions at the Intercosmic Space Program in Wisconsin. I just figure that when the aliens take over Earth, and they catch us again, we'll be fed to that bioship. I'm not up to going through that again."

The professor took his used cotton handkerchief from his vest pocket. "Is that possible, Ray? Will we be able to use Pegasus to get to Wisconsin?"

Ray swayed back and forth, as he adjusted to the movement of the motorhome barreling down the dirt road. "To be perfectly honest, it's a long shot. First of all, the liquid methane we'll get out of an LNG tanker will not be pure. Second of all, Pegasus will be hauling a lot of weight," he said, looking at the professor with a smile. "But on the upside, we're only going to Marinette, Wisconsin, and I can maneuver Pegasus next to Infinity One. If we were to fly an airplane, we'd have to land further away."

"Not to mention the fact there's probably nowhere to land because the planes are probably scattered all over the runway, just like the vehicles on the highway are," Max said. "But if we can't find a tanker to transport the fuel to Pegasus, then our mode of transportation will have to be the motorhome or a plane."

The professor pushed back the recliner, resting his thick legs on the footrest. "Using the motorhome would expose us to more radiation from the nuclear power plant meltdowns. We'll spend many hours, possibly days, in the radioactive fallout. Pegasus has the ability to shield us from radiation." He clasped his fingers behind his head, as if ready to fall asleep. "Are you able to drive Infinity One, Ray?"

Ray smiled. "I was one of the test pilots and it's a magnificent craft. They've kept it top secret, leading to a lot of the UFO sightings. It's far superior to any ship so far known to mankind."

"We hit the jackpot rescuing you," Max said, looking at Ray still dressed in his orange flight suit.

"Whatever we decide to do, we only have three days to do it," Father said, placing a foam-filled box pillow behind his back. "And three days happens to be Christmas Eve."

"I'm glad it's too warm for snow," Tony said, following the road through the Huron National Forest. "Otherwise, we'd need a snowplow to get down this road if things were normal."

"Normal," Max grumbled, leaning forward with his elbows on knees. "What I wouldn't give for that; snow or not."

"In case anyone's keeping count," Father said, "I think the fourth seal, mentioned in the Book of Revelation, has opened."

He had everyone's attention. The professor opened his eyes. Tony looked into the rear-view mirror as Jack turned in his seat to face Father. Ray's smile disappeared and Max looked at Father with eyes magnified behind the lenses of his glasses.

"The fourth seal is the fourth horseman. The horse is a pale horse—actually, it's a sickly green color in Greek—and its rider is Death and Hades. It's believed to be the worst of the four horsemen because it's a combination of the riders before it. So one fourth of the earth will die from violence, famine, pestilence, and even wild beasts."

"I hope those damned killer seagulls aren't coming back," Max said, rolling his eyes.

The professor hacked into his handkerchief. "You know I'm a man of science, never been a believer in all this hocus-pocus religion stuff, but I must admit, Father, there may be something to it."

"So how many seals did you say there were?" Tony asked, glancing back at the gray-haired man of God who was wiping his sweaty palms on his black trousers.

"There are seven seals," Father said. "There are the four horsemen, then souls under the altar, then wrath of the Lamb, and finally, the seventh seal where there is silence. That is, before the seven trumpets are blown. Then there is hail and fire, a mountain cast into the sea, darkness, plagues, angels released on the earth, and then the final trumpet praises God. With the sequence complete, the divine judgment is complete. So it's out with old, and in with new."

The professor hacked again. "Well, I was being converted until you said all that. I don't want to get into a religious discussion about all this, but what kind of a God does this to his people?" He stuffed the dirty hanky back into his pocket. "I'm going back to my old way of thinking."

"If what you say is true," Ray said, catching his balance as the motorhome slowed. "We still have a lot to go through. It also strengthens my vote for getting to Infinity One."

"We're coming to a crossroad," Tony said, stopping at the intersection. Just as at the compound, the alien moss covered the trees, causing limbs to break and dangle from trunks like flies caught in a pink spiderweb.

"Take a left," Jack said, looking at the map. "It should take us into Mio. It doesn't seem to be a very large town, but it should have a couple grocery stores."

"Do you see a natural gas processing plant?" Max asked.

Jack studied the map. He flipped it around, refolded it, unfolded it, and then handed to Max. "I don't know; you figure it out."

With a huff, Max took the map and studied it. "Looks like there's one east of here at Au Sable, on Lake Huron. I can't tell if it processes LNG or just receives shipments from waterborne vessels for transport. Either way, we may find a tanker truck there."

"There's probably no power at the plant," the professor said. "But I'll assume they have a natural gas generator keeping the power on and the storage tanks cold."

Ray moved to a chair in the galley. "That's right. As long as the LNG is kept at a constant pressure and steam is allowed to leave the tank, the temperature will remain at minus two-hundred-sixty degrees. It's called auto-refrigeration."

"Is that shit explosive?" Jack asked, looking at Ray.

"When methane, or natural gas, is in a liquid state, it won't explode because it doesn't contain oxygen. But the vapors are flammable when they mix with the air and there happens to be something to ignite it," Ray said, looking through a drawer next to the table. He pulled out a small fast-food packet of salt. "Anyone want some?"

They shook their heads.

"Let's load up with food, gas, and supplies first," Tony said, turning left on the road. "Then we can go get that fuel."

FOUR

Tony kept driving as fast as he could, navigating around fallen branches that were in the process of being digested by the moss.

"Professor, will that moss shit digest us like it's digesting the trees?" Jack asked, turning his seat to the side.

The professor had fallen asleep in the recliner. The movement and vibration of the motorhome, as it rumbled down the dirt road, had put him to sleep like a baby being rocked in a cradle.

"Professor, wake your ass up," Jack said. "We're almost in town and I want to know if that moss is going to eat us."

The professor yawned and leaned forward, pushing down the foot rest. It took him a minute while he looked out the windows and the moss blanketing the landscape. "It did have phagocytic properties, like white blood cells that consume foreign material. From the looks of the crumbling landscape, they have gotten stronger as they've grown. They appear to be devouring Earth's vegetation at a rapid rate and increasing in size."

"So are you saying they can eat us?" Jack asked, wanting a yes or no answer.

"It's possible. That could be what was causing the sores on some of the preppers." He looked around at the others. "Does anyone have blisters or wounds of any type?"

Everyone looked at their arms and at each other's faces. No one showed signs of being eaten.

"I suggest we stay away from it," Max said, looking at the dense pink clumps of plants engulfing trees, bushes, and lawns. Even the buildings and the road were covered with a thin carpet of the creeping plant. "At least the buildings aren't on its list of favorite foods . . . at least so far."

Tony slowed and drove down the main street, past a bank with a loan sale sign; an ice cream parlor with a picture of a three-foot high vanilla ice cream cone; a dry goods store, and various other small businesses. There were no people walking on sidewalks, or shopping for Christmas gifts. In fact, the town had died a couple months ago as Halloween ghosts and goblins still adorned shop windows rather than Christmas lights and Santa Claus.

Max stood up and walked to the small bathroom. While he looked at his tired reflection and stubbly beard in the mirror over the sink, Tony drove into the disordered parking lot of the Mio Market. Just as every other place they had been, cars sat abandoned, doors remained open, and grocery carts rested against fenders.

"We still have to watch for zombies and tornens," Tony said, pulling up to the entrance. He turned off the ignition and stood. "Do you still have your pistol, Professor?"

The professor patted his hip holster. "I don't think Randy's thugs knew I had it. My vest was long enough to cover it."

"That Vin kid took mine," Father said, showing the empty shoulder holster under his black clerical jacket.

"I know Max doesn't have a weapon," Tony said, running his tongue over his teeth as if he had a toothpick between his lips. "Since Jack has the alien handgun and Ray has the M16, they can go in the store and get the supplies while I start siphoning gas. Professor, you and Father stay here and guard the RV." He looked at Max returning from the bathroom. "You should help get supplies, just stay close to Jack and Ray."

Tony opened the door and moved into the stairwell. He had his rifle raised as he stepped into the thick air and then promptly sneezed. "It feels like pollen season out here."

The professor followed Jack, Max, and Ray out the door, stopping on the last step. "It's spores, not pollen. The moss is reproducing." He stepped back inside and closed the door.

"I don't see anything moving," Tony said, taking two gas cans and a siphon hose from the trailer, next to the all-terrain vehicle. "Let's make it quick."

With Jack in the lead, Max in the middle, and Ray covering the rear, the three men walked in the side door of the grocery store. Except for the light spilling in through the windows on the face of the building, it was dark and quiet. They did not have to pull grocery carts from the line in the store; instead, they each claimed an abandoned cart from the aisle.

Jack walked to a flashlight display. "Get flashlights and batteries; fill your carts with food and whatever will make the preppers happy, and then we'll split."

Max struggled to open the flashlight package. A couple minutes and a couple plastic cuts on his fingers later, he finally released the handheld lights. He put the batteries inside and lit his path as he pushed his wobbly-wheeled cart behind Jack while Ray went down the next aisle. Lettuce, broccoli, and green beans lay rotting in warm, humid chillers. A rotten potato, inside a ten-pound bag, gave off the odor of a rotting mouse. He looked over at the deli with its cold cuts and salads, there was going to be nothing edible in there. He slipped, catching his balance before he fell on the hard tile floor, next to defrosted freezers that had emptied their melted content.

"Damn it," Max said, steering his cart out of the puddle toward the row of rancid meat. When he looked at the butcher area, it brought back memories of Father Mitch strapped to a meat saw by one of the crazed kids they had the unfortunate luck of running into while in Kalamazoo.

He watched as Jack began depositing cans of whatever food he happened to be walking by into the metal basket of his cart. Max shined his flashlight at Jack's selection of supplies. "Ketchup, mustard, and pickles? Jack, I don't know about you, but I don't want a bowl of mustard for lunch. We should be getting things like soup, tuna fish, and beans."

Jack shined his light at Max's empty basket. "At least I'm gathering food." He walked up to the coffee and dropped the large metal can into the basket. "Do you think you could step it up a bit, Max?"

"I think you should stop dropping things in your cart, you might wake one of those things up. If I remember correctly, the heads of those tornen are pretty tough."

They both shined their flashlights to both ends of the aisle, there was nothing creeping up to them.

Jack frowned. "Let's just hurry it up. We should get as many of these carts filled and in the RV as fast as we can."

By the time their carts were full, they had an assortment of grocery items, including dog food. Ray was leaving the store with his cart by the time Jack and Max got up there. Max held the doors as Jack pushed both carts through and into the pink haze.

"Did the spores get thicker or are my eyes playing tricks on me?" Max said, pushing his cart to the open motorhome door.

Jack coughed. "It's definitely thicker."

The professor and Father quickly took the food and packed it into the bedroom, not concerning themselves with neat stacks or order of any kind.

"Keep it coming," the professor said, "and don't forget bottles of water."

They raced with their grocery carts back into the store as if they were playing a television game show where contestants were required to fill their carts with items on a grocery list while looking for bonus items in which to reach the required total of groceries in a short amount of time. Indeed, they were racing against the clock, but it was not a shopping spree and there were no bonus prizes.

Tony entered the motorhome, rubbing his itchy, watery eyes. "Those spores are kickin' my ass."

"Looks like you're allergic to them," the professor said, helping Father move food to the back of the coach. "I'd stay out of them for a while. Maybe they won't be so bad when we get by Lake Huron."

"I hope so," Tony said, taking a wad of tissue from a box on the cab console. He hacked up sputum and spit it onto the white tissue. "It's pink."

The professor had just sat down when Ray brought another cart of groceries. "If that vaccine hadn't have warped the preppers thinking, they could have come here and gotten their own food; they have their own vehicles and weapons."

Max stood by the couch, watching Ray toss items through the door, along with cases of bottled water. A jar of pickled pig's feet rolled toward Tony's feet, followed by a jar of grape jelly. Ray looked at Father and smiled. "Sorry for the mess and the pig's feet, but I know The Community loves them and I want to be on their good side." He closed the door and sprinted back inside the store, the grocery cart bouncing in front of him.

"I wonder if the aliens eat pickled tornen," Tony said, pushing the jars, with the side of his combat boots, toward Father. Then he picked up the map Jack had been looking at. "Looks like it'll take an hour or two to get to Au Sable."

Father picked up the jars and looked at the professor. "How is your supply of blood pressure medicine? Do you need more?"

"No, you guys got me enough on the last trip to last at least a year," the professor said, watching Father as he carried armfuls of food to the overflowing bedroom.

Father unloaded his arms and leaned against the galley counter. He looked at the pile of cans and jars scattered everywhere. "You know; this would go a lot faster if you two helped."

As the three tired men gathered up the food, Ray and Jack had returned with two more full carts.

"I think you boys can stop," the professor said, plopping down in the recliner, squeaking from his weight. "If the preppers want any more, they can get it themselves. I'd like to get to the fuel for Pegasus before it gets dark; you know how there's always something that happens to put a crimp in our plans."

Ray and Jack went inside the motorhome and helped carry items to the rear, while everyone else looked toward the store, waiting for Max to push the last load through the doors.

"Well," Tony said, turning his cab seat to see the professor. "I think our trip just got its first kink. Where's Max?"

FIVE

"I don't think you need to cry about it," Jack said, watching Tony wipe his eyes. "Ray and I will go get him."

"I'm not crying," Tony said, and then he blew his nose. "I've got a bad case of hay fever . . . I mean, spore fever. I'm allergic to those spores floating in the air."

"No shit," Jack said, looking at Tony's watery eyes.

"I'm nominating Ray as our new driver," Tony said, as tears continued to drip from his eyes. "I can't see through these tears, everything is blurry. I want someone who can see where they're going."

"You got it," Ray said, climbing into the driver's seat.

Father stopped trying to organize the cans and jars and looked through the galley window toward the entrance. "What's taking him so long? I think someone had better check on him because he doesn't have a gun."

"I'll go," Jack said. "Ray, you stay here and get ready to tear out of here."

"No problem," Ray said, looking at the dashboard.

Jack gripped the alien handgun as he stepped out of the motorhome, closed the door, and listened. There was no sound of Max shouting for help, only an occasional hiss, or maybe it was a wheeze. It sounded like it was far enough away so that he could walk to the store entrance without worry of being attacked by something.

Spores from the alien moss, that seemed more like floating seeds than the single-celled reproductive bodies that Max said they were, filled the air like miniature snowflakes. Jack walked to the entrance through spores that were now piled an inch or two high on the pavement.

When he got inside, he heard hissing coming from the freezer area. Raising his weapon, he walked toward the sound. When he reached the aisle, he saw two tornen at the far end, looking at the glass display case and running their slimy fingers along the doors, leaving streaks of mucus. In fact, mucous covered their bodies as if it was oozing from pores in their leathery amphibian colored skin. That must be what made these legless creatures slide along so well at the hospital. Their long, muscular arms could easily drag their slippery torsos over the ground, he thought.

Jack knew their skulls were hard because bullets were deflected when he had shot at them in the health center's lobby. He would need to aim for what appeared softer tissue and the heart. Then, he thought, he did have an alien weapon, it could probably kill them in an instant, but on the other hand, he had never shot a tornen with it. Maybe his alien weapon would not work on an alien creature.

He quietly and slowly inched forward, stopping when he saw Max inside the case, scrunched between shelves of sticky melted ice cream. Apparently, the tornen did not know how to pull open doors. Otherwise, Max would have been a bony appetizer for the ugly beasts, barely whetting their appetites.

Then he saw Max notice him, his wide-open eyes seemed to take up a good portion of his face as his glasses magnified his eyeballs. Jack could not shoot at the tornen because Max would also be hit by the gun's ray beam. He would need to lure them away, but where to? He knew they could run surprisingly fast with only two arms.

Before Jack had time to decide where he was running to, one of the tornen noticed him.

"Run to the RV," Jack shouted as he shot back down the aisle and in the opposite direction that Max needed to go to get out of the store.

He ran toward a long open chest in the center of the aisle. It was once refrigerated but now held rotting hamburger and pork steaks. Jack could hear them almost on him as the boots he had taken from a zombie lost traction and he fell forward. He turned on his back and fired without aiming, there was no time. The ray from the gun cut a path through the air above him, striking the first tornen, and then the second, dropping them on top of him.

Adrenaline surged through his body, giving his muscles the energy they needed to allow Jack to spring up, turn around, and aim the alien gun at the nonmoving tornen. He was breathing heavy, ready to pull the trigger, but it was not necessary. He stood there a moment, looking at the dead, or stunned, tornen. He lowered the weapon to his side as he backed away enough to feel just a little safer. The tornen skin had brown warts like a toad, and oddly, smelled like vanilla.

Jack tucked the handgun back in the waistband of his jeans and slowly jogged to where Max had been. He was gone. Footprints of sticky cream headed toward the door until they disappeared. Jack ran out the front door to the motorhome. He went inside and saw Max taking off his wet, sour milk work shirt, revealing a build so scrawny he could be taken for a prisoner of war who had been fed only seaweed and soybeans.

"What are you looking at?" Max said, frowning. He rolled up his work shirt and T-shirt, tossing them in the corner as Ray drove away from the store and through the parking lot.

Jack held back a laugh. "Good thing you're a scientist, Max."

"I need to know which way to go," Ray said as he pulled onto the road. "Someone needs to read the map for me."

"I can't read it," Tony said, lying on the couch. "I can't stop my eyes from tearing."

"I'll read it," Jack said, sitting in the passenger seat.

"I need clothes," Max said, sitting across from Father at the galley table. "Unless you guys want to hang around me smelling of sour milk . . . and whatever other odors may be emanating from my clothes, I suggest we at least stop somewhere while we're in town."

"Actually," Father said. "Socks and underwear for me isn't a bad idea, either."

"There should be a clothing store on this main stretch," Ray said, slowing the motorhome as he drove past cars that had collided with each other.

Jack looked up from the map and watched as Ray maneuvered around automobiles. The spores were still floating through the air, swirling upward as Ray drove through them. The afternoon sun reflected on the pink spores, making them glitter as if they were in an apocalyptic snow globe. Then he saw clothes in a store window and a black and white sign that read, Rebel Wear. "There's a store."

Jack looked over at Ray as he stopped the motorhome. "That's a Goth store."

Max walked to the front. "You picked a Gothic clothing store? I'll look like some kind of vampirish punk."

Jack turned and looked at Max. He did feel sorry for the frail man, but clothes were clothes. "Do you want clothes or not? We don't have all day to find you a store with janitors' work clothes."

Max shook his head, raised his arms in defeat, and walked back to the table. "Just don't come back with black fingernail polish."

Jack stood up and took the handgun from his waistband. "Professor, you man the driver's seat. I want Ray to come with me so we can get this done in less than fifteen minutes."

"Not a problem," the professor said. His chair creaked as he leaned forward and moaned as he stood up. He walked to the driver's seat. "I could use some clean underwear, too. I think we all smell a little ripe."

SIX

Jack and Ray returned with two large shopping bags full of clothing.

The professor was beginning to abandon the driver's seat when he saw a streak of yellow buzz through an intersection ahead. "Shit, I think I just saw a yellow Hummer speed through that intersection."

"What? I wonder if that could've been those crazy kids," Jack said, walking up to the cab, sitting in the passenger seat.

The professor stood and waddled back to the recliner. "I don't know who it was, but we're not the only people in the area . . . unless zombies can drive cars."

"Shit, Jack," Max said, going through the clothes in the bags. "Couldn't you find something that won't make me look like I'm going to a funeral?"

Jack turned around and saw Max putting on a black T-shirt with a skull on the front and the message: Life in Death. Jack laughed. "I think you found your style."

Max grumbled as he pulled out a black hooded sweatshirt, slipped it on, and pulled up the hood. "Now I look like an assassin."

Ray got into the driver's seat. "Where to?"

"Take a left at that intersection," Jack said. "Hopefully, we don't run into those kids. I'm sure they still have weapons and they didn't like us much last time we saw them."

Ray turned on the window wipers and then turned them off. "Those spores are making it hard to see, not to mention making the road slippery."

"Just don't put us in the ditch," Max said, zipping up the jacket.

Ray drove out of town, following the paved road and the Hummer's tracks. "Any idea why those kids would be going the same direction as us?"

Jack shook his head. "No idea. I'm surprised they're even up here. I just hope they're not going to the same place we are."

"Why would they want rocket fuel?" Father asked, taking his turn looking through the bags.

"Maybe it's not LNG they want," the professor said. "That processing plant probably has propane they can use to cook and heat with."

"Speaking of propane," Father said. "Maybe we could also take a tanker of propane back to The Community. I don't think they're going to be very happy with us pulling up with a tanker of liquid methane to fuel the spacecraft."

"I didn't think of that," Jack said. "So let's see; Ray can drive the LNG tanker, and," he paused and looked at Tony still lying on the sofa. "Can you see, yet, Tony?"

Tony blew his nose. "No, and my nose is stuffy and my throat is scratchy," Tony said, with a nasally voice. "We got to get away from these spores, they're killing me. I'm basically useless at this point."

"Shit, that's not good," Jack said. "Okay, that leaves me to drive the propane truck and one of you three to drive the motorhome." Jack leaned back in his seat and clasped his hands behind his head. "We'll have ourselves a convoy."

While they rolled along the spore-covered road, still following the tracks of the Hummer, Jack messed with the radio, turning its dials through channels of static. "I don't think there's much life out there."

Ray slowed the motorhome to forty-five miles per hour, as the spores were now around six inches deep. "The spores just keep piling up. I hope this downpour of moss cells eases up so that we're able to drive back to the compound. Otherwise, we'll need to find a truck with a snowplow to cut a path for us."

"We're going to run out of drivers, pretty soon," Jack said.

Ray continued driving through the unrelenting spores while everyone either closed their eyes for a snooze or stared out the windows, watching the spores cover the landscape like volcanic ash.

Father would pick up stray cans of beans and fruit cocktail as they occasionally became dislodged from the jam-packed rear of the motorhome. They would roll toward the front of the coach like bowling balls searching for a tenpin strike. Instead, they found either Tony's foot that he had over the side of the couch or the back of the cab's seats.

"We're almost to the processing plant," Rays said, startling everyone awake or to attention. "And I hate to tell you, but that Hummer is going to the same place we are."

Jack held the alien handgun in his hand. "Everyone, be on the lookout for those kids."

"Their tracks are going inside the plant," Ray said, heading toward the open gate. "I'll veer away from them as soon as we get inside; fortunately, this place is huge."

"I hope you know where you're going," Jack said, looking at the tall processing towers, an odorant injection station, and storage tanks. And what appeared to be, miles of pipelines winding around each other like a 3D maze.

"I'm heading for those three large storage tanks over there," Ray said, pointing toward three round concrete containers, each around eighteen stories high and about as wide as a football field. He steered the motorhome the opposite direction as the tracks he had been following.

While the spores continued to rain down upon them, they drove slowly past the gas and liquid separator pumps, the gas sweetening towers, and dehydrator tanks. It was as if they were in an extraterrestrial city, where alien technologies produced its own energy and oxygen for life under a dome.

"I saw the Hummer," Father said, moving closer to the window. "It's on the other side of all these . . . things, and they're going our direction."

"They probably saw us, too," Jack said. "But I don't think they know it's us because we didn't have the motorhome the last time we saw them."

"I see two LNG tanker trucks by one of the storage units," Ray said, driving toward the liquid methane. "The propane is probably on the other side, exactly on the opposite side of where we're headed."

Then a loud crack echoed through the metal containers and towers, causing everyone to jump.

"Shit, what was that?" Max said, crouching in his chair.

"It sounded like gunshot," Ray said, stopping the motorhome. "Were they firing at us?"

"I don't think that's a good idea to be shooting a gun around all this gas," Max said, wishing they had found an army surplus store with bulletproof vests, rather than black apocalyptic attire. "Those nitwits are going to kill us all."

SEVEN

Clare was leaning against the headboard of a bed on the second-level bedroom of the Cartwrights home, reading a dog-eared paperback of Little House in the Big Woods, by Laura Ingalls Wilder. Sarah was seated by the bedroom window; watching members of The Community go in and out of the hospital. Sarah had not ventured outside the Cartwrights home since the men were sent away, but she assumed the people going in the hospital were busy having their skin wounds tended to.

Sarah listened to the kids—Willis, Georgie, and Dawn—play with Jibber and Miss Foo in the next room. "I feel like I'm in jail."

Clare looked up from the book. "We are."

"And I'm so hungry my stomach is cramping," Sarah said, looking over at Clare, who had put her book down and was sliding toward Sarah.

Clare whispered, "They took my gun and your wand. But if we could get to that shed where they have them locked up, I bet you could just zap them all to sleep like you did that gorilla in the hotel."

"Or kill them. You know I don't know exactly how that thing works, other than it reads my thoughts. Maybe one thought of harming them would trigger it to kill them," Sarah said. She stood up and began to pace the room while Clare took the window seat.

"Maybe we can break into the shed and get our weapons," Clare said. "That guy who took control of The Community from Cecil lives over there. I'm sure he has a key."

"And exactly how are we supposed to get it from him?" Sarah said, still pacing to relieve her anxiety. "And if we do get the key and get our weapons back, then what? We can't leave this place. Am I supposed to keep knocking them out for three days?" She rubbed the back of her neck. "It sounds risky to me. Besides, what if the guys are getting everything the preppers told them to get and their back here in a day or two; and the preppers live up to their promise and we're back in their good graces. If we break into the shed, get our weapons, and harm The Community . . . well, who knows, maybe they'll hurt us. They are rather unpredictable."

Clare sighed. "I suppose, but let's keep the option open because you never know what the future holds. Especially if the guys run into a problem and don't make it back here by Christmas Eve . . . or they don't bring the right food, or whatever."

Sarah nodded. "Yeah, I'll keep the option open."

"Do you want your seat back?" Clare said, watching Sarah walk back and forth.

"No, I'm going to the outhouse," Sarah said, walking toward the bedroom door. "I'll be right back."

"Too bad we're banned from the indoor plumbing," Clare said, shaking her head. "We're just not worthy of any of the power the wind turbine generates, I suppose."

"Yep," Sarah said, as she walked out of the bedroom and into the hallway. She listened to see if Mr. and Mrs. Cartwright were in the house before going down the stairs, she did not hear any sounds coming from the lower level of the house.

When she reached the living room, she saw no one. An afghan blanket lay neatly folded on the top of the couch and the pine floor appeared swept and dirt free. She looked into the bathroom. It was tempting to just sneak in there, do her business, and leave; but the Cartwrights would find out. Somehow, they would know.

She walked into the clean kitchen, free of dirty dishes in the sink and plates on the counter. She noticed a small loaf of bread dough left to rise on the dining room table. Then she saw it, next to a folded dishtowel—syringes. Four syringes, two empty, and two filled with an amber liquid.

"Oh my God," she said with a hushed voice. "They've started taking the vaccine again. I can't believe even the Cartwrights have fallen for the misguided advice of one of Randy's thugs."

Sarah walked up to them for closer inspection. She picked up one of the empty syringes and saw trace amounts of the vaccine at the needle hub. She sat it back down where she had found it and stood there not believing what she was seeing. The steady stream of people in and out of the hospital must have been them receiving the vaccine. Now what? Are they going to get even crazier? What about the weird bone deformation, is that going to get worse?

She wanted to run up and tell Clare, but she had to go to the outhouse first. She walked out the front door and onto the porch. A few spores floated in the air, but not many. She noticed people watching her as she walked to the outdoor toilet. She lifted the latch and walked inside, closing the door behind her.

She could hear people talking but could not make out what they were saying. For a moment, she wondered if Randy's thugs would force the vaccine on her and the others. It would be easy to overpower them, one at a time. The thought of people standing outside the latrine made her afraid to leave as she looked around for the toilet paper. There was none.

"Damn it," she said. "They won't even let us have toilet paper."

There was nothing to wipe her bottom. All she had was a small tissue she had kept in her jean pocket when she left her home a couple months ago. She had never thrown the used tissue away, thinking it could come in handy some time. Now was the time. She wiped and zipped her pants.

Sarah unlatched the door and stepped out, the air was beginning to fill with more floating spores as a circle of community members surrounded her. She stopped, unable to return to the Cartwrights house unless someone moved out of her way. She quickly looked at their hands, fearing they had needles ready to jab into her.

Then The Community's new self-proclaimed leader, Daniel, stepped forward, blocking her path to the Cartwrights house. He had an M16 in one hand and a syringe in the other.

EIGHT

While the spores rained down upon them, two young teen boys, with colored bandanas over the lower half of their faces, stood in the haze with hunting rifles pointed at them.

"That's those crazy Buddy and Vin kids," Jack said, looking through the motorhome window as his jaw tightened. "They're far enough away that I don't think they recognize us." He looked at Ray. "Do you mind volunteering to talk with them and see what they want?"

"I don't think I'm volunteering, but sure, I'll talk to them." Ray took a deep breath and looked at Jack. "Is there anything I need to know about them?"

"Yeah," Max said, staying away from the window. "They're nutty and can't be trusted."

"That's right," Jack said, nodding in agreement. "Just tell them we're here for the methane, not the propane, and then we'll leave."

"How many are there?" Ray asked, climbing out of the driver's seat.

"There are four of them. The oldest boy is around fifteen and his name is Buddy. Then there's Vin and a girl named Jewel," Jack said. "There's also a little kid who looks like he's in first grade, his name is Half-Pint."

"That little one has my Bowie knife," Tony said, stomping his foot.

"You sure know a lot about them," Ray said, picking up his M16. "I'm taking a power stance on this; I don't want to look like an easy target."

Jack nodded. "Sure, whatever you want."

"Toss me up one of those grim reaper hooded sweatshirts," Ray said. "I want to look like someone who shouldn't be messed with."

Father reached into a shopping bag and handed Ray a black Goth garment.

Ray put it on and pulled up the big droopy hood. "If I had time I'd put on the full Goth getup." He turned toward the others. "How do I look."

"You look like Death except you're not a skeleton and you're carrying a rifle instead of a scythe," Max said, looking at Ray's stubble beard in the shadow of the hood.

"Here I go," Ray said, opening the driver's door. He stepped out and walked toward the kids who were still standing, side by side, watching him.

They anxiously watched as Ray stopped several feet away from the kids who appeared to be carrying on a conversation.

"If they take him hostage, like the preppers did you, Tony, I'll shit my pants," Jack said, keeping his face in shadow. "Especially since Ray's the only one who knows how to handle that liquid methane."

"The kids are walking away and Ray's coming back," Father said, letting out a sigh of relief.

Ray opened the driver's door and climbed back inside, followed by a puff of spores. Everyone looked at him, waiting for him to speak.

"Well, what'd they say?" Jack asked, leaning forward with a hand on the knee.

Ray pulled back the hood and looked at Jack. "They are here for the propane truck, just like we thought."

"Why'd they let you leave without a gunfight?" Max asked, sitting upright once again.

"Well, because I told them . . ." Ray began and then let his words taper off.

"You told them what?" Jack asked, looking up at Ray.

"I told them we were here for the liquid methane and that it was nothing they could use," Ray said. "But one of the kids said the processing plant belonged to them and that I didn't have permission to take the LNG."

"So are we getting the methane or not?" the professor asked with a sharp tone.

"Now we are," Ray said, keeping his head bowed.

"So what did you say to them to get their so-called permission?" Jack asked.

Ray cleared his throat. "They told me I had to pay them or they'd kill me and then they'd be over here to kill all the rest of you next."

"Yeah, so, what did you say?" Max said, getting annoyed. He smacked his hand on the dinette table. "Don't tell me you told them they could have the food?"

Ray kept his head bowed. "They wanted the motorhome. I had to give them the motorhome. They'll be over here shortly to get it."

"No frickin' way," Jack said, tensing up. "Those damned hooligans are not taking the motorhome and the food. I'll stun their frickin' asses if they come over here."

"What were you thinking, Ray? I thought you were taking a power stance," the professor said. "We need to get this food back to the preppers so that we can get the rest of our group and get the hell out of there."

"I believed they were going to kill me," Rays said, still standing just inside the door. "They had their guns pointed at me and their eyes . . . I'm sorry." He kept his head bowed.

"Don't get down on Ray," Father said. "Any one of us would have done the same thing. Those kids were going to saw my hands off . . . remember? They probably would have shot him, and us, too."

"Jack, get ready with that alien gun," Max said, cowering back down in his seat. "They're on their way over here right now."

NINE

The longest night of the year was leaving the processing plant in near darkness as the kids walked over with guns and flashlights in hand. Jack opened the passenger window just enough to allow the alien handgun's ray beam free passage to the outside as he squatted between the seat and the dashboard. "Quick, dim the interior lights."

Buddy and Vin stood outside the motorhome door with raised guns. They shouted, "Everyone, out of the RV."

Jack looked over at Ray, who was beginning to stand. Then Jack jumped up, pointed the gun out the window, and pulled the trigger. Nothing happened; the gun did not fire. "Shit." He pulled the trigger again, but the gun still would not fire.

Vin saw Jack and immediately fired his rifle at him. A bullet lodged in the side of the cab, only inches from Jack's torso.

"Stop shooting," Ray shouted as he walked to the door. He looked down at Jack and whispered. "What happened? Why didn't it fire?"

Jack shrugged. He wanted to shoot again but with Ray about to open the door, he did not want him to be the next target.

Ray shouted through the door. "Put your weapons down before we come out."

"No way," Buddy shouted back. "You just tried to shoot us. Everyone out, now!"

"Tony, are you able to see yet?" Jack whispered.

"No, my eyes are swollen shut," he said, still prone on the couch. "There could be a safety lock on it, but I don't remember seeing one when we were practicing with it."

Jack held the handgun next to a light underneath the dash. "I can't tell."

"You and Ray can overpower them," Tony whispered. "Make a big deal out the alien weapon, they'll probably be afraid of it and then you can tackle them."

"Let's do it, Ray," Jack said. He got up and stood next to Ray. He looked back at the professor who was taking the pistol from his hip holster.

Another shot rang out and another bullet lodged in the side of the motorhome.

"Get out here, now," Buddy shouted, again.

"Someone should go out the driver's door, go around the RV, and cover them," Tony whispered.

"I'll do it," the professor said, sliding his overweight body forward on the recliner seat. He walked toward the driver's seat and was about to open the door when another shot cracked through the air.

"They're trying to come out the driver's door," a girl shouted.

"Kill 'em if you have to," Buddy said.

Ray looked at Jack, who gave a nod. Ray flung open the door and both he and Jack had weapons raised at the boys.

"Jewel," Buddy shouted. "Get over here."

Ray and Jack were about to be outgunned when the professor heaved his weight through the door, pointing his pistol at Jewel.

"Drop your guns," Jack demanded.

"Drop yours," Vin said. Then he laughed when he thought he recognized Jack. "You look familiar. Are you those people who invaded our Walmart?"

Then Half-Pint walked around the other side of the motorhome, holding out Tony's Bowie knife.

"Max, take my rifle and get out there," Tony said.

Max grumbled. "I'm getting pretty sick of all this gun fighting." He dropped to his trembling hands and knees and crawled over to the couch where Tony had the rifle extended. "Act like you know what you're doing."

"Yeah, right," Max said. He stood, pulled back his shoulders, and walked out the door, taking aim at Half-Pint.

Buddy smiled. "Well I'll be, it's the mechanic."

Vin laughed, then said, "Shit, you're right. But there's also a military dude and a priest. Where are they?"

"The spores have made them sick," Max said, trying to act with authority even though he felt like running away and hiding.

"We're not giving up the RV," Jack said, keeping aim on Buddy. "Have you noticed what I'm holding?"

"Yeah, you got that gun from the aliens," Buddy said.

Vin laughed uncontrollably.

Jack kept it pointed at Buddy, surprised he knew what it was. Did they have contact with aliens just like

Randy and his thugs? "It's powerful and can kill you. So I'd hightail it out of here if I were you."

"Go ahead," Buddy said, holding back a laugh. "Fire it."

Jack did not want to pull the trigger just in case it killed them, but he did anyway. Nothing happened. He squeezed the trigger again. The alien gun was useless.

"It won't work on us," Buddy said. Still keeping the rifle pointed at Jack. Then he cocked his wrist. "As long as we have these bands on, that weapon won't hurt us."

Jack recognized the band as being the same band he had slid on Randy's wrist, preventing him from leaving the alien spaceship. Otherwise, he would have exploded if he had continued forcing his way inside Pegasus. But the band was shielding the kids. It must have more than one purpose. "Do you know what else that band does?"

Vin stopped laughing long enough to say, "And you do? So tell us, what else do these bands of protection do?"

Jack was happy to explain. "The aliens put those on people they take as prisoners, trapping you on the spaceship, keeping you from escaping." He was thrilled to point out the next fact. "And they'll make you blow up if you try to escape. Did the aliens give them to you?"

Vin's laugh subsided. "He's lying."

"How do you know about the bracelets of protection?" Jewel said, keeping her rifle aimed at the professor.

Jack was still happy to explain. "Because we were on the alien spacecraft and they take humans as prisoners, making them work for them, and they even feed humans, and other living creatures, to their bioships. We are fuel for their ships and slaves for them."

"Is that true, Buddy?" Jewels asked, sounding afraid as her voice quivered.

He did not answer as he studied Jack. "I wasn't told that."

"Why would they tell you?" Jack said. "They wanted you to put the bands on and then they'll come back for you when it's time. Go ahead, try and take them off."

Half-Pint began working on his band, forgetting about standing guard on Max. He began to panic as he slid the Bowie knife into his boot so that he could use both hands to pull on the band. "It's true, it won't come off."

Jack watched as Half-Pint continued pulling his band, he was distracted and now an easy target. He looked over at Jewel, who was now working on her band. "I can't get my bracelet off either." She began to cry. "They lied to us; the aliens lied to us."

When Buddy and Vin saw Jewel and Half-Pint struggling to pull the bands off their wrists, they began tugging on theirs. No one was able to slip them off their wrist.

Jack seized the moment. "I suggest we work together, against the aliens, and stop shooting at each other. The aliens are tricksters, here to take over the world."

The unrelenting spores kept falling to the ground, now in piles six inches deep. The kids were now more concerned about getting the bands off their wrists than with targeting Jack and the others.

"The spores are getting deep," Jack said, lowering his gun. "I suggest we call a truce and get what we came here for and then get out of here before the spores are too deep to drive in."

"Let's get the propane and get out of here," Jewel said, walking away.

Buddy and Vin watched as Half-Pint ran after her.

"Just stay out of our way," Buddy said, as he and Vin began walking toward the Hummer. The beam from their flashlights made the spores sparkle as the kids became blurs in the dark, thick air.

"Let's get that methane before those kids change their minds," Max said, ready to collapse from fright.

"Get in the RV and I'll drive us to the LNG," Ray said, turning toward the door.

Everyone got back inside the motorhome as Ray began driving toward the huge storage containers. The headlights barely penetrated through the spores, but there was enough light to see two LNG cryogenic tanker trucks parked next to a transfer station with flexible stainless steel hoses.

"Is the liquid methane still good to use?" the professor asked.

"It should be," Ray said, parking so that the motorhome's lights shined toward the tankers. "As long as the pressure has been constant, the temperature of the LNG should be constant. Those tankers are like thermos bottles and should be able to keep it cold for weeks."

"I'll go with you," Jack said, putting the handgun in his back waistband and picking up a flashlight.

"I'll take the helm," Father said, moving into the driver's seat.

Jack followed Ray to the first tanker truck and watched as he wiped the spores from the gauges and shined his light on the dial faces.

"This tanker is almost full," Ray said, examining the rest of the instruments.

"Is this going to be enough fuel to get us to Wisconsin?" Jack asked,

"For Pegasus, it is," Ray said. "Especially since we're not leaving Earth's atmosphere. The older engines would burn around five-hundred-forty gallons of fuel per second to get the craft into space, but we don't need to worry about that."

"Does Infinity One use methane?" Jack asked, following Ray to the cab.

Ray climbed into the cab of the tanker truck. "No, it uses something entirely different."

A distant truck powering on caught Jack's attention. He looked in the direction of the kids and saw a blur of lights drive away, followed by the Hummer. "Looks like those kids got the propane truck they were after. They're leaving, I'm going over and see if there's another one."

Ray started the truck, closed the door, and rolled down the window. "Hop on and I'll drive over to where they distribute propane."

Jack jumped on the truck step and held onto the grab bar as Ray put the big rig in granny gear and began pulling the double-walled, insulated, cryogenic tanker. Jack waved for the motorhome to follow them as Ray crawled toward where the kids had taken a propane truck.

The spores, still raining down like cottony seed hairs from a cottonwood tree, made it difficult to see further than a hundred feet. If it were not for scattered emergency mercury-vapor lights illuminating critical plant operating areas, it would be near impossible to navigate through the processing plants several acres, as evening darkened the sky.

Ray stopped the rig when the lights shined on metallic wire mesh cages filled with various sized propane cylinders. Five-gallon bottles for grills, up to the tall twenty-five-gallon cylinders for heating, stood inside the storage cabinets.

"I don't see any propane trucks, but those bottles will work," Ray said to Jack through the truck door's open window.

Jack jumped off the step, slipping on the slimy spores as he walked up to the cages. He tested the door on each cage and found them all locked, except for the one housing the smaller five-gallon bottles. He opened the door and pulled out two of them. "Let's get these and get the hell out of here," he said, walking past Ray toward the motorhome's trailer.

Ray got out of the truck and took another two propane cylinders to the trailer where Jack was securing them next to the ATV. He looked at his feet. "There has to be eight inches of this shit. You should drive the RV and I'll follow you before we get snowed in with the stuff."

Jack nodded and tested the bottles, making sure they were secure. "Let's go."

TEN

Sarah stopped and looked at Daniel who was blocking her path. "What's going on?" She already knew what was going on; they were going to force her to take the BW vaccine.

Daniel smiled as he held up the syringe. "It's time for you and the others in your group to abide by The Community's rules and accept the BW vaccine."

There was no way she was taking the vaccine, and no way would she allow them to inject the others. However, she wanted to stay calm and not irritate the members of The Community, who circled around her, keeping her from running. Was Clare watching? If so, was she able to come to her rescue? Sarah had no idea. Besides, the preppers had taken their weapons and she had nothing to fight with, except her words. "Daniel," she said, softly. "We are not members of The Community and we will leave here and not take any more of your food and supplies . . . as soon as the men get back."

"She lies," John said. He raised the M16 and pointed it at her. "They are planning to overpower us and take control of The Community. Besides, Daniel, they are a threat to our wellbeing while they walk around not protected by the vaccine." He spit on the ground, now covered with a fine layer of spores. "They will likely turn into zombies or some other monster, and kill us all."

"That's not true," Sarah said. "We would have already turned into zombies if that were going to happen. Surely you realize that." Her heart pounded. "The vaccine has side effects and you're not thinking right." She thought about what the professor had said about its side effects. "It could kill you if you keep taking it."

The group surrounding her tightened the circle. Daniel raised the syringe and approached her, stopping a few short feet in front of her. She could smell him. He had the same sick odor that she noticed on Randy when they were on Mars. He reached for her arm.

Sarah backed into the people behind her, panicked. "We'll leave, we'll leave now and you'll never see us again . . . I promise."

"You can't leave," Daniel said, jutting his already protruding chin. "When your men return, they won't think kind of us just letting you leave. You and your people need to stay here so that the men are guaranteed to leave the food without causing a ruckus . . . then your clan can leave and never return."

The people behind her had grabbed hold of her arms, not allowing her to run away, something she was desperate to do. Then she thought she would try a different approach. "Since we are using your supplies, why do you want us to take the vaccine, something I'm sure you only have so much of. Why give your valuable doses to us? Especially when we'll be leaving soon."

Daniel laughed. "You and your kind think you're so smart. We do not have a limited supply of the vaccine. We make it ourselves. We made sure we had that capability to manufacture biological warfare defenses when we moved into the compound, and that includes the vaccine."

Sarah looked around for Cecil and the Cartwrights, but they were nowhere to be found. She tried to break free from the preppers grip, but they held her tight as Daniel grabbed the deltoid muscle in her upper arm, ready to plunge the needle and its contents into Sarah's body.

ELEVEN

Clare dropped the book she was reading when she heard Sarah scream and people cheering. As she ran to the window, she heard the shouts of encouragement turn to piercing cries of fear. She saw Sarah surrounded by a mob of deranged people.

Clare ran out of the bedroom, shouting for the kids to stay put in their room, as she ran down the steps and to the kitchen. She grabbed the butcher knife that Mrs. Cartwright had thought she had hidden, and ran out the front door toward Sarah. "Let Sarah go," she shouted, extending the broad-bladed knife toward the others.

For a moment, Clare thought she had intimidated the others with her weapon as she watched some of them run back to their houses. That was until she heard kids running from Lake 66 toward the compound's central square shouting, "The zombies are crossing the lake."

The Community abandoned Sarah, leaving her standing alone by the outhouse. Clare ran up to her. "What happened?"

Sarah wiped tears from her eyes and looked at the syringe lying in the sand. "They tried to give me a vaccine. They're crazy."

Clare was not sure what to think. Sarah was rubbing her arm and sobbing. She hugged Sarah, trying to make sense of what was happening and how they could defend themselves. Then she said, "Did . . . did they do it? Did they make you take the vaccine?"

Sarah stopped crying and lifted her sleeve to look. She rubbed her arm. "I don't think so. Everything happened so fast, but I think it was knocked out of his hand when everyone charged out of here."

Clare reached down and picked up the vaccine; fluid still filled the barrel. "You got lucky; it doesn't look like he had time to inject you." She took the needle into the outhouse and dropped it into the toilet pit.

Sarah and Clare looked toward the lake. It was difficult to see, because of the distance, but it did indeed appear as though someone, or some things, were crossing the lake in rowboats.

"It's going to take a while for them to reach us," Sarah said, taking in a deep breath.

"Now we just have to figure out how to get our weapons out of that locked shed," Clare said, looking toward the outbuilding.

"Reasoning doesn't work so well with them," Sarah said, beginning to walk back to the Cartwrights house.

Clare wrinkled her nose. "I have an idea what may work, but I'm not looking forward to it."

"What?" Sarah asked, stopping in her steps as she looked at Clare.

Clare shook her head and sighed. "I'm going to use the oldest profession to entice that wacky Daniel to let us have our weapons back."

Sarah stared at Clare. "No way. You're not talking about what I think you're talking about, are you?"

Clare continued walking back to the house. "Don't worry, I'm not really going to do anything with him, but he doesn't know that."

They stopped short of the porch. "It's too risky. The vaccine has them not thinking right and he might . . . take advantage of you."

"I can defend myself," Clare said, putting her hands on her hips.

"It's a bad idea, but . . .," Sarah said, letting out a deep, weighted sigh.

"Do you have a better idea how to get our weapons?"

Sarah shook her head and walked onto the Cartwrights porch. When she tried to open the door, it would not budge. "I think it's locked."

Clare reached up and knocked, but no one answered.

Sarah walked over to the dining room window, but the drapes were pulled shut. She rapped on the window. "Mrs. Cartwright, it's Sarah, can you let us in?"

There was no answer.

Clare took her camo cap off, ran her fingers through her hair, letting it fall softly around her face. She was about to put the cap back on when she decided to hand it to Sarah, instead, along with the butcher knife. "I'll be back."

Sarah took the cap. "What? Now?"

Clare whispered, "Watch the shed; I'm going to try and get the key from Daniel. We're running out of time."

Sarah did not say anything as Clare walked off the porch. She followed her off the porch and walked far enough from the house so she had a view of the kids' bedroom windows. All the curtains in the house were drawn. She looked back at Clare, who was walking to Daniel's house. Then she looked at the small building where Max kept his telescope; she would wait in there and watch for Clare to signal her. The kids would need to fend for themselves until Clare was able to get their weapons back.

TWELVE

Clare walked through a gentle flurry of spores as she approached Daniel's door. She stood in front of it, fluffed her hair with her fingers one more time, and knocked. She saw him look through the window and heard him walk toward the door.

Daniel opened the door. He smiled. "Are you here for the vaccine?"

Clare put on a fake smile. All she wanted to do was smack his greasy face. But instead she said softly, "Daniel, as you know, I'm skilled with weapons and can help defend The Community from the zombies crossing the lake." She glanced toward the beach, and what appeared to be three rowboats filled with zombies, rowing their way toward them. "Soon they'll be here."

Daniel laughed. "Good try; you're not getting your guns."

Clare fumed inside. Of course, as she expected, Daniel would not give up the weapons easily, even if it meant helping him. She forced herself to look coyly at his round protruding eyes while teasingly rolling her hair over her fingers. Soft and seductively, she said, "I was thinking . . .

maybe . . . we could work out a deal." She watched as he smiled and watched her. "Do you know what I mean?"

Daniel leaned against the doorframe and crossed his arms. "Maybe you need to spell it out for me."

Bastard. She looked down shyly and then back up at him with a coquettish grin. "My husband is gone, and I'm willing to . . . make an exchange."

"Spell it out, babe."

He was an ass but appeared to be taking the bait. "This for that. Quid pro quo, if you know what I mean." She wet her lips with her tongue, partly to make them moist and a little more enticing, but mostly because her lips were dry from The Community denying them sufficient water.

Daniel stared at her for only a moment before opening the door all the way and motioning for her to go inside.

She stepped in and saw John and some other Community members sitting around, watching. She was outnumbered; this was not going to work. She moved back to the door. "We need privacy."

"What's going on Daniel?" John said, leaning back and putting his feet on the coffee table. "Don't trust her, Daniel." He snickered, and then said, "But I'll take her off your hands if you want me to."

The men in the room laughed as Daniel followed her outside and closed the door behind him.

Clare turned toward him as the falling spores stuck to his balding head. She reached up and flirtatiously brushed it from his oily scalp. "We have to make this fast because the zombies are coming."

"What do you propose?" He moved close to her.

She had caught him, now to real him in. Clare moved her face next to his and whispered in his ear. "The shed with the weapons, that makes it fair." She brushed against him; this moment would decide the outcome.

He stood there, letting her stay next to him. Then he reached into his pocket and pulled out a key. "Let's go." As they turned and walked toward the shed, he grabbed her arm tightly. "No funny business."

Clare briefly winced at the pressure of his grip; the vaccine did not seem to have made them weak. She did not say anything as they approached the shed door. While Daniel unlocked it, she looked across the courtyard and spotted Sarah watching. Then she looked back at the lake, the zombies were still on their way. She would need to make it clear to him that her getting the weapons would help him.

"The zombies are getting closer," she said, watching him open the door.

Daniel motioned for her to go inside first. "We'll need you at the beach to pick them off before they have a chance to reach shore."

She nodded and motioned for him to go inside first. She did not want to step in ahead of him because for all she knew he would close and lock the door behind her. "After you."

Daniel took Clare's hand and pulled her inside the dark shed with him. The sun was setting and the spores filtered any remaining light, but she saw Sarah's purse first, and an array of various weapons, most were not from their group.

Her heart raced and her faux smile was difficult to maintain as she watched Daniel look at her, waiting for her to continue the vampish part she was playing. She had only seconds to decide what to do before Daniel became angry. She did not see her .44 Magnum revolver. Then she thought, even if she had seen it the preppers probably had removed the cartridges. But Sarah's purse likely still held the wand and it needed no ammunition.

Daniel got between her and the door. "What's wrong, having second thoughts?"

"No," she said, making sure she kept the hook in his mouth. To buy herself a little time she slowly removed her vest. While he watched, she looked for Sarah's purse again; unfortunately, she would have to get past Daniel to reach the wand. "Your turn."

He snorted a chuckle. "You like to play games, do you? Okay, but you didn't take off much. But considering the zombies are almost upon us, we need to speed this up a bit."

As Daniel began unbuckling his belt, she ran past him, picked up Sarah's purse, and reached inside feeling for the wand. She did not find it.

THIRTEEN

Randy was reaching for Clare's neck when Sarah burst through the shed door, wielding the knife's sharp blade in front of her.

"Back off, Daniel," Sarah said, her voice sharp and determined.

Daniel held Clare's neck tightly with one hand and his pants up with the other. "You're both whores and should be treated as such." He was angry, gripping Clare's neck with such force her face was turning red.

Sarah watched her purse drop to the sheds dirt floor as Clare reached up, trying to pry Daniel's sweaty hands away from her throat. Sarah reached down, picked up her purse and took the alien wand from an inside compartment. She held it close to Daniel, only a couple feet away. She thought of just touching it to him, fearing that if she shot a beam at him it would also affect Clare.

While Clare gasped for air and Daniel squeezed her throat, she reached forward and touched his arm as if she were using an electric cattle prod. Daniel immediately stumbled backward, falling against shelves of hammers, nails, and wrenches. His knees buckled and he fell to the dirt as Clare inhaled deep wheezy breaths.

"This is ridiculous, Daniel," Sarah said, her voice quivered. "The zombies will be here soon and we need weapons to fight them. We need to work together on this . . . or we all die."

Daniel was on his hands and knees, looking at Sarah and Clare as if he were a bull, ready to charge. He snorted snot from his nose as he spoke. "A witch and a whore, you both should be hung." He looked around and picked up one of the hammers that had fallen next to him. "As leader of The Community, I charge both of you with treason for betraying the members who so kindly protected and nourished all you infidels."

When Daniel used the word infidel, it immediately reminded Sarah of her time on Mars and the creatures in the corral and Randy, who worked for the aliens. It made her think, or rather, realize that Daniel also worked for the aliens and that he was their chattel, just like Randy said that he was. Sarah was not sure whether to feel sorry for him or kick dirt in his face. He seemed pathetic with his thinning hair, protruding bones, sunken cheeks, and bulging eyes. Randy had said that he had the choice of either working for the reptilians and half-breeds as slaves or be fed to the bioships. They lured him with a honey pot, promises of power over humans and creatures, along with a bounty of food, and women for the taking. Apparently, the aliens do not stand by their promises since Clare so easily seduced him. Nevertheless, he took the vaccine and has likely been doing whatever the reptilians and half-breeds told him to do.

Sarah followed his gaze. He was looking at Clare's .44 Magnum revolver, it apparently had fallen in the commotion. She did not take her eyes off him as she waited to see if he was going for it. He did.

"Good night, Daniel," she said, shooting a golden beam of light at him.

He fell on his face, a pile of bones covered with greasy flesh.

Sarah saw his shoulders rise and fall. "He's alive, but he'll be out for a while."

"Quick, let's gather the weapons and ammo. I'll go to the beach while you check on the kids at the Cartwrights." She put the revolver in her holster and then touched her red neck. "Sound good?"

Sarah looked at Clare's neck. Red lines in the shape of Daniel's fingers wrapped around her throat. "Are you okay?"

"I'll be fine," Clare said, forcing a painful swallow. "Take Georgie's sword with you."

Sarah looked at the sleeping Daniel. "What should we do with him?"

"I'd take him to the jail if we had time," Clare said, picking up her vest and shaking off the dirt. "I'd like to just close the door and maybe the zombies won't find him. But we should tell his cronies to come get him."

When they walked out of the shed, it was almost too dark to see. The sun had set on the horizon and the spores in the air had thickened.

Clare looked toward the lake. "It's getting too dark to see. I'll go to the Cartwright's with you and we'll just hold tight there."

"I think I hear them," Sarah whispered. "They're almost here."

"We'd better warn everyone," Clare said. "I'd yell, but my throat is not in any condition to do it."

Sarah shouted as they walked to the Cartwrights house. "Everyone, stay in your houses. Barricade your homes because the zombies are almost here." She paused and then shouted toward Daniel's house, "John! Daniel is in the shed; you'd better get him. Plus, the zombies are almost here and someone should be manning the shoreline."

FOURTEEN

Sarah handed Clare back her camo cap and the butcher knife as John and a few others ran out of their houses toward the beach with guns in hand. Cecil and another prepper went to the shed and pulled Daniel out, dragging him back to Cecil's. They walked up the porch steps to the Cartwrights front door and tried to turn the knob. It was still locked.

"Now what do we do?" Sarah asked. "They still won't let us in."

Clare wrapped on the door window loudly. "Let us in or we'll break the window."

"Your voice sounds horrible. I'll do the talking," Sarah said. "With the way the Cartwrights are acting, I'm thinking it's best we don't stay here and maybe stay in the guard tower."

"Good idea," Clare said, walking off the porch. "Let's get the kids out of the house and go there, it'll be easier to defend." She reached down, picked up a pebble and walked around to where the kids' bedroom was. She threw it at the window. It clinked against the pain of glass and then fell to the ground.

Sarah followed Clare and looked up at the bedroom windows closed curtains. "You'd think they'd be looking out and watching us."

"I'm wondering if the Cartwrights have done something to them, like have them locked in a room somewhere or even have them tied up," Clare said, looking for any movement behind the glass. "Looks like we're going to have to break-in and get them."

The zombie's moans were growing louder. It was as if they were trying to shout, but instead, wails of pain echoed through the darkness. Shots from the lake's edge cracked, startling both of them.

"We have no time to waste," Clare said, running back to the porch. "Use your wand and see if it'll break through the front door."

Sarah walked to the porch steps and pointed the wand at the front door. Nothing happened. She concentrated harder; using her thoughts was the only way she knew how to use the device. "I can't tell if it worked." She walked up the steps to the front door; it was still locked. "Maybe it only works on living things."

"I doubt it," Clare said, walking up next to her. "That's a powerful weapon, it should work."

Sarah looked along the porch and saw a concrete flower pot with dead flowers in it. She picked up the heavy container and handed it to Clare. "I'll let you have the honor of breaking in."

Clare took the weighty soil-filled container. "Stand back." She lifted it shoulder height, close to her neck and threw it at the door's glass window as if she were putting a shot. The flowerpot caused the glass to crack, but not break.

"That glass is tougher than it looks," Sarah said.

Clare picked up the container that had rolled back toward her when it hit the floor. This time, with greater force, she threw it at the window as hard as she could, expelling a huff of effort as the formed concrete broke the window and landed on the kitchen floor.

Before approaching the door, they both listened, not wanting to be shot or killed in any manner by their loud breaking and entering in progress.

Clare went to the door and used the butt of her revolver to bust out jagged pieces of glass where she needed to place her arm when she reached inside.

"Do you see or hear anyone?" Sarah asked, standing behind Clare.

"No," Clare said, reaching her arm through the opening. She turned the lock's knob, pulled her arm carefully back out and opened the door.

They walked inside and crept past the concrete flowerpot that had rolled by the sink. There was no sound and no people.

Sarah looked at the dining room table where she had earlier seen two full, and two empty syringes. Now there were several empty syringes sitting on a clean white cloth. "Clare, look," Sarah said, alarmed. "Did they give the kids the vaccine?"

"I sure as hell hope not," Clare said. She looked at the needles and walked into the living room, both hands gripping the raised gun. "Is anyone here?"

"We need light," Sarah said, walking to a kerosene lamp sitting on a writing desk, next to a notepad. She searched through the bureau's drawers and pigeonholes until she found a box of wooden matches. She lit the lamp and adjusted the wick so that it cast the most light into the room. Then she picked it up by the wire handle and followed Clare.

They walked through the living room, where Sarah expected the Cartwrights to be sitting in their usual chairs; Mrs. Cartwright in the rocking chair and Mr. Cartwright lying on the couch.

"Where is everyone?" Sarah asked. The only sounds she heard were the hiss of the lamp and Clare calling out for the kids.

"Let's go upstairs," Clare said, approaching the steps.

"Willis, Georgie, Dawn, where are you?" Sarah shouted as they began ascending the stairway.

Sarah kept looking behind them as they climbed to the landing, waiting for the Cartwrights, Daniel's thugs, or zombies to be coming up behind them. Aside from occasional gunshots from the beach, the house was like a tomb. They walked to the kids' room where the door was ajar. Clare pushed it open with her foot and walked inside. The kids and dogs were not there.

"Where did everyone go?" Sarah asked, looking around the room for anything the kids could have left, possibly a note or a message.

Clare lowered her revolver. "Let's check the rest of the rooms up here, downstairs, and the basement. They couldn't have gone far."

Sarah walked to the window and looked toward the beach. The preppers had spotlights shining over the lake, aimed at the zombies rowing toward shore. Through the thin layer of fog hovering over the still water, zombies could be seen falling from the boats and into the water after being shot. Were they sinking to the bottom of the lake or were they swimming underwater like sharks looking for arms and legs to rip from bodies and then devour. "We'd better find the kids soon because I have a strange feeling that some of those zombies are going to make it to the shore."

"I agree," Clare said, walking out of the room.

Having found no sign of the kids upstairs, they headed back downstairs. They searched the bathroom, laundry room, and a spare bedroom.

"Does this house even have a basement?" Clare asked.

"I don't think so," Sarah said.

"Where else could they be?" Clare said, watching shadows dance on the walls from the flickering light.

"I didn't see anyone going out the front door while we were busy with Daniel," Sarah said. "So let's go out the back door and see if we can find them."

They walked out the back door and looked around. It was like a ghost town. People had their houses darkened and shutters closed. The spotlights being used to illuminate the man-eaters were beginning to shine unsteadily.

"It won't be long and the floodlights will be dead," Clare said, watching the preppers' fire continuously at the approaching boatload of zombies.

"I sure wish the men were here," Sarah said, standing close to Clare.

"Me, too," Clare said. "Not only for more gun power but because I want to get the hell out of here."

"Are we going to have to go back inside the house?" Sarah asked, looking back at the dark building.

Clare sighed and shook her head. Then she saw a faint flicker of light behind the churches stained glass windows. "The church, let's try that first."

They ran toward The Community's house of worship, stopping momentarily to see if the possessed people were making it to shore. So far, the preppers were holding them back.

"They should be able to take all those zombies down," Clare said. "I only saw three rowboats of them, how many zombies could there be?"

"Oh my God, Clare," Sarah said, almost dropping the lantern. "There's a zombie coming out of the water. Is it possible that some swam across the lake?"

"They could be the ones that fell from the boats after being shot, and are still . . . alive, or whatever you want to call it," Clare said. "But no matter if that's the case or there's a bunch of them that swam across alongside the boats, we're screwed."

"I don't think screwed is a strong enough word," Sarah said, running up the steps to the church door. "We're dead."

FIFTEEN

Sarah tried to open the door, but as she expected, it was locked. Both she and Clare began banging on it.

"Let us in," Sarah pleaded, pounding her fist on the wooden door. "Mrs. Cartwright, please let us in. You know we don't mean you or anyone harm. We just want the kids."

The door was still locked.

"We'll break a window and make you vulnerable to the zombies who are coming ashore," Clare shouted with authority. "You have ten seconds to open this door or I'm throwing this . . ." she paused and looked around for something to throw. Then she saw two three-foot high sculptures—resembling a grotesque representation of reptilian aliens—standing guard at the church entrance, like gargoyles protecting a medieval building.

Just as Clare picked up one of the statues, they heard the lock click and saw Mrs. Cartwright opening the door.

"Quick, get inside," Mrs. Cartwright said in a scathing tone. Her disdain for them was obvious as she glared at them, ready to grab them and force them to move.

Clare and Sarah went inside and stopped. Mrs. Cartwright closed and locked the door and walked away from them, standing next to Mr. Cartwright and several other unhappy Community members.

Panic washed over Sarah. It was not caused by the sight of the group of deformed members staring at them, one being Cecil with an M16 rifle pointed their way. But rather, it was the sight of the kids tied up and gagged with duct tape over their mouths, behind the altar.

"What's going on here?" Sarah asked, looking at Mrs. Cartwright, who was looking sickly. The skin around her bulging eyes was darkening, as was everyone else's in the room. Even though the light cast from the lanterns in the room was warm, it nevertheless made the citizens of The Community look jaundiced as if the BW vaccine was damaging the liver.

Two of the men began approaching them with ropes in their hands. But they stopped when Sarah raised the wand toward them and Clare kept her revolver pointed at the man with a rifle.

"Sarah," Mrs. Cartwright began. "There is much you don't know about The Community."

Sarah watched Mrs. Cartwright walk over to the kids who were struggling to break free from the restraints. "Why do you have the kids tied up?" She pointed the wand at her, wanting to will it to fire but the kids were too close to her. "Untie them, now."

Mrs. Cartwright smiled as Mr. Cartwright stood beside her. He cleared his throat, thick with phlegm. "We cannot release them until the zombies have left."

"Why?" Sarah said as she pointed the wand back toward the men trying to approach her with the ropes. They stopped.

Mrs. Cartwright extended her arms in a gesture of openness. "My dear Sarah," she sighed. "I suppose we might as well tell you." She reached under the altar table, brought out a crucifix, and placed it on the crisp white linen cloth.

Sarah looked at the cross; it was strange. The crucified body was not that of Jesus Christ, but instead, it was a reptilian alien. She could not believe her eyes, but it was so. "You worship the aliens?"

"It's a long story," Mrs. Cartwright said, watching her husband tip a bottle and pour an amber liquid, with the consistency of honey, into a gold chalice.

Sarah trembled as she remembered the liquid. It looked like the same liquid that the half-breed alien Rausuca tried to get her to drink before raping her at the nuclear power plant. The thought made her angry, so angry she felt like willing the wand to kill the Cartwrights and all of the people of The Community.

Clare noticed Sarah's reaction. "Are you all right?"

Sarah did not answer, she kept watching, just like the Cartwrights wanted her to do.

"Sarah," Mrs. Cartwright said. "Please do not be angry with us, we only want to protect our members."

"You people are crazy," Sarah said. The words came out rushed as adrenaline surged through her body.

"Don't be so judgmental," Mrs. Cartwright said, with an air of superiority. "You would do the same if you were in our shoes."

Sarah's breathing increased and her heart pounded. She did not trust these people.

Mrs. Cartwright continued, "We had to make a pact with the heavenly brothers. In exchange for preserving the lives of our families, we agreed to allow them to modify the elderberry component in the biological warfare vaccine. And to work for them, assisting them with tasks more suited to humans, allowing the heavenly brothers to carry on with their noble duties."

"Heavenly brothers?" Sarah said. She was so angry she could hear the blood pounding through the vessels in her ears. "Are you talking about the aliens?"

Mr. Cartwright reached under the altar table and brought out a gold paten filled with dried elderberries. "I suppose," he said, gently placing it beside the chalice. "We owe our survival to them and will do anything they ask. They have protected us, but the unfortunate many that turned into zombies could not be avoided. Soon the heavenly brothers will return to Earth and all evil, hardships and ill health will be gone. Gone forever."

Sarah wanted to tell them how ridiculous it was and that the aliens were lying to them, but she did not want to anger them. "That doesn't explain why you have the kids tied up. If everything is so grand, why are you doing this?"

"Well," Mrs. Cartwright began as she lit a candle on the altar, "we do not totally trust the heavenly brothers . . . sad to say. We were born preppers and we need to protect ourselves if the zombies happen to break inside the church."

"It's just precautionary," Mr. Cartwright said, keeping his attention focused on the altar table items. "We have the church marked as a safe area, but if they happen to get in, we'll need a diversion, something to appease the zombies. An offering I suppose you could say. The kids are the sacrifice."

"No frickin' way," Sarah said. A bitter tang filled her mouth. She wanted to run up and strangle them both.

"Why aren't all The Community members in here?" Clare asked. She glanced at Sarah, who appeared ready to fight and then looked back at Cecil still aiming the rifle directly at her. "I'd think they'd all be running in here for safety."

"They're workers, a class below us," Cecil said, cocking his head. "The heavenly brothers only granted those of us with a pedigree to sit at their communion table."

Then Sarah watched as Mr. Cartwright reached under the altar and take out a tray with dozens of syringes neatly stacked on top. He placed it next to the paten while Mrs. Cartwright placed a black stole around his neck, letting it hang down in front.

Keeping her revolver aimed at Cecil, Clare slowly stepped to a side window when the sound of people screaming and a barrage of gunfire began echoing outside. She looked out long enough to see the chaos. She gasped. "There are dozens of zombies running through the compound. We need to secure this building before they get in."

"The building is secure," Mrs. Cartwright said, dismissively flipping her wrist.

Clare looked at Sarah and whispered, "Use that wand and put everyone to sleep."

Sarah nodded. While Mr. Cartwright spoke a prayer in a language that sounded like something that would be spoken in Egypt or a long lost ancient culture, she willed for the wand to put everyone to sleep. Nothing happened. She concentrated harder, but again, nothing happened. "It's not working."

Cecil laughed as he watched them. "That won't work in here. As we said, the church is protected."

Clare whispered to Sarah, "It worked against the aliens at Palisades, so I'm thinking there must be a blocking device somewhere in the building. Probably behind that locked door where they won't let even Father go."

"Then we have to get in there," Sarah whispered, still keeping the wand fixed on the men with the ropes.

While mayhem reigned outside the church, Mr. Cartwright calmly raised the chalice and sipped the nectar. He handed it to Mrs. Cartwright who did the same. Then Mr. Cartwright picked up a syringe while his wife pulled up her sleeve. She closed her eyes while Mr. Cartwright whispered a prayer as he gave her an injection of the vaccine. She opened her eyes and in turn gave him an injection, making the ritual appear as though it belonged in a church of Satan.

Sarah whispered to Clare, "We have to do something."

While gunshots cracked and blood-curdling screams continued outside the church, Clare whispered, "There's only one person with a gun. I don't want to shoot Cecil, but I'm going to have to."

Sarah nodded.

While people began to line up for their turn to receive the vaccine, Clare whispered, "When he looks away and is distracted, I'll shoot his leg and then we'll run up and take the M16 from him."

"Sounds good," Sarah whispered. "Hopefully, we can get into that room . . . the sacristy."

"We'll get in there one way or another," Clare whispered, shifting her weight and getting ready for action.

"Make it fast . . . while they're distracted," Sarah said.

The muscles in Clare's arms were growing fatigued as she kept the revolver raised and aimed at Cecil. She was not sure how she was going to wound Cecil and shoot him in the leg when he was standing in front of the pews, blocking the lower part of his body. She did not want to kill him or even give a life-threatening wound. All she wanted was to graze his leg, causing a distraction that would make him move his focus from her to his injury, so she could run up and take his weapon.

"He won't stop staring at us," Clare whispered. "We need a distraction so that he looks away."

Sarah thought about what she could do to cause a distraction without getting herself shot in the process. She whispered, "I'll use the banned movie theater phrase."

Clare nodded, keeping her eyes fixed on Cecil, who was staring back.

Sarah took a deep breath, pointed toward the back of the church, and shouted, "Fire!"

Panic broke out causing Cecil to turn and look to where Sarah was pointing. That was enough time for Clare to run up and push the muzzle of her revolver into the back of Cecil's balding, buttery scalp.

"Don't move," Clare said, sounding like a Drill Sergeant demanding discipline; all she needed was a boonie hat to replace her camo cap.

Sarah ran up and grabbed the M16 from Cecil's shaking hands as the men with the rope ran toward the sacristy door. She pointed the gun at the Cartwrights.

"You people," Sarah said, pointing the rifle at The Community members. She was so angry she felt like she could be frothing at the mouth. "Get against the wall and turn around."

Everyone, except the Cartwrights, looked confused as they obeyed her, walking between the pews to the wall of stained glass windows.

"Put your hands over your head," Sarah shouted.

Clare pushed Cecil away from her. "Stand with the others."

Cecil moped as he passively walked away.

"See what that vaccine is doing to you people," Sarah said, feeling like she was hyperventilating. "It's causing you to not think right. And you, Cecil, used to be the one Community member who was rational, now you're . . . sick from the vaccine."

"Open that door," Clare said to the Cartwrights, "and then get over with the others."

The Cartwrights stood at the altar smiling.

"Why do you want in the sacristy?" Mrs. Cartwright asked, acting like a meek little mouse. "There's nothing in there for you."

"Just open it," Clare said, moving toward them, "and get away from the altar."

While Mrs. Cartwright clasped her hands in front of her, Mr. Cartwright reached under the altar.

"Don't move," Clare said, moving behind them and the drape covered table. "Raise your hands and get over there with the others."

Mr. Cartwright began pulling his hand from between the drapes.

"What's in your hand?" Clare asked, keeping the gun pointed at him.

He showed her his empty palm while Sarah began untying the kids.

"Both of you, with the others, now," Clare said.

While Mr. Cartwright began walking to the wall where the other members faced, Mrs. Cartwright paused and said, "It's not wise to go into the sacristy because it is keeping a force field around the church and is keeping those things from getting inside. If you are wise, you will leave it be."

Sarah had untied Dawn and was removing the duct tape from Georgie's mouth—who still had his hand-and-a-half sword in its scabbard—while Clare moved the drape underneath the altar table.

"I'm surprised they didn't take your sword," Sarah said, moving on to Willis.

Georgie rubbed the red skin around his mouth where the tape had been ripped. "Everything happened so fast." He took the sword from its sheath and examined its shiny blade. "I think they believe it's a toy."

A click came from the locked door.

"I think I just unlocked it," Clare said, walking from the altar to the sacristy door. She looked at the Cartwrights who were standing next to the rest of The Community members.

"We have to get the dogs," Willis said, immediately as his gag was released.

"Where are they?" Sarah asked, untying his hands.

"I don't know," Willis said.

"We'll find them," Sarah said, walking to a window. It was dark outside and difficult to see. Nevertheless, she saw movement around the church. Dark shadows accompanied by moans; the zombies had them surrounded.

"Don't go in there," Mrs. Cartwright said, watching Clare put her hand on the door lever.

Clare pushed down on the handle and pulled the

door open.

SIXTEEN

Jack slowed the motorhome to forty miles per hours. Spores were still raining from the sky, leaving a slippery slime on the road as the RV's tires pushed through several inches of the reproductive cells. He looked at the side mirror and saw the smudgy glow of the tanker truck's headlights following him.

"This shit just won't stop," Max said, from the passenger seat. Then he turned his attention to the map he had spread on his lap. "Don't go too fast, Jack, I don't want to miss our exit. It should be coming up."

Jack squirted more washer fluid on the streaked front windshield. "This slimy stuff is worse than a buildup of ice. All the wipers do is smear the gunk around."

"Just watch the road, Jack," Max said, nervously. "I don't want to end up in the ditch."

Jack looked over at Max, who was looking at the map with trembling hands. He glanced back at Tony, who was still laying on the sofa, the professor in the recliner, and Father who was walking up from the galley.

"How are things going?" Father asked, holding on to the back of Max's seat.

"I think I need to go out and clean this mess off the windows," Jack said, squinting through the besmeared window. "I'm having a hard time seeing."

"I saw a squeegee in the closet," Father said, turning to walk back to get it.

"I think that's our exit up there," Max said, pointing toward nothing recognizable, other than the coating on the glass.

Jack put the flashers on and gradually slowed to a stop. "I'll clean the windshield before we go any further."

Father returned with the long handled rubber-edged blade from the closet and handed it to Jack. "Do you need help?"

Jack opened the driver's door. "No, you guys stay in here."

Tony sat up, rubbing his watery eyes. "What's going on?"

"Jack's just cleaning the windows," Father said, watching Jack walk to the front of the motorhome. Then he turned to look at Tony. "Are you feeling any better?"

Tony shook his head, sneezed and lay back down. "No, I feel like shit."

"Here comes Ray," Max said, looking out the side mirror.

Moments later the motorhome's door opened and Ray stepped inside.

"What's going on?" Ray asked, shaking spores from his boots.

"Had to stop and clean the windows," Max said, turning his seat to look at Ray. "Can you see out yours?"

"Not really," Ray said. He stood in the stairwell, not wanting to track the organisms still attached to his boots, inside the coach.

The professor stood up and walked to the cab. Then he looked at Ray's pant legs. He took a tissue from the console and wiped some of the pink spores from Ray's flight suit. "I still can't get over how large these spores are and how fast they germinate."

Max leaned forward, pushing his glasses up his nose as he focused on the spores that Jack was having difficulty removing from the windshield. "These aren't just spores on the windshield; they appear to be a mass of spreading moss. They're even growing shoots. We'll be covered in a clump of moss and stuck to the road if we don't get moving."

The professor looked back at the spores in the tissue. "I'll be damned. They appear to be moving freely like an animal, just like my experiments have been showing."

"So what does that mean, exactly?" Father asked, walking over to look at the life forms in the tissue.

"It means," the professor said, as he crumpled the tissue and stepped past Ray so that he could toss it out the door. "It means that if this plant has animal characteristics, then it can move freely and has a highly developed nervous system." He walked over to the hand sanitizer in the console and squirted a dollop into his palm. "It also means that it doesn't make its own food like a plant can, so it will need to . . . feed on something."

"Like what?" Ray asked, his voice cracked. "Like us?"

The professor shrugged. "Who knows."

Max turned in his seat to look at the professor. "If that damned moss starts growing mouths with teeth, I want to go back to Mars."

Ray laughed. "I'll be right behind you."

The motorhome door opened and Jack stepped inside, setting the squeegee in a corner. "I don't know what's up with those spores, but they're holding onto the RV for dear life, plus there's at least a foot of that stuff on the ground, now." He walked back to the driver's seat.

"Hurry up and get us to the compound so that I can refuel Pegasus before she's buried in a pink mat of that stuff," Ray said, opening the door.

"You're preaching to the choir," Jack said, putting the motorhome into drive.

Ray stepped out and ran back to the tanker truck.

Jack saw the truck's headlights flash. "I think he's ready." He gave it gas, but the motorhome spun it wheels, unable to move forward. He put it in reverse, but he could not back up. The tires whirred on the pavement as they spun. "We're stuck."

Father opened a galley drawer and took out a steak knife. "We may need this to cut the moss."

Jack looked back at Father. "Cut the moss? You think it's growing that fast?"

"It probably is, Jack," the professor said. "It has animal characteristics and may be able to think . . . maybe even intelligently."

Jack groaned. "You've got to be kidding."

"I'll take it, Father," Max said, grumbling as he walked over to get the serrated table knife. "I'm taking your rifle, too, Tony."

"Go for it," Tony said, wiping tears from his eyes. "I'm getting rather pissed off that I'm stuck her on the couch, like a helpless . . . something."

Max handed Jack the knife, took one of the flashlights, and followed him out of the motorhome.

Jack shined a light on the front wheel. "That stuff has already grown up the tire." He knelt down and cut its slimy stems, releasing its grip from the rubber. He and

Max worked their way around the motorhome, cutting the moss that was holding the tires to the road.

"Let me see that moss," Max said, shining the light on a clump that Jack had ripped from the tire. "It looks like it has veins."

"And blood," Jack said, dropping the wet stems. He wiped his hands on his pant leg and they got back inside the motorhome, where Father was had a tub of baby wipes open for them to use.

"Did you cut yourself?" Father asked, looking at Jack's hands and pant leg.

Jack looked at the red fluid on his hands. "It's from those plants."

"Let me see it before you wipe it off," the professor said, standing. "Moss typically is nonvascular, but this moss has vessels . . . blood vessels."

"I'm glad I can't see," Tony said.

"The aliens are really pissing me off," Jack said, using one of the moist towelettes to wipe the substance from his skin. "I'm going to wring Rausuca's neck the next time I see him."

SEVENTEEN

When Clare opened the sacristy door, The Community members began shouting at her to not turn off the power shield.

"Don't touch anything or turn anything off," Mrs. Cartwright said, having now lost the contemptuous smile she had while at the altar. "The power shield encapsulates the church building and protects us."

The gunfire had subsided outside. Clare was not sure if that meant the preppers had killed all the zombies or the zombies had killed the preppers. But what she did know was that the zombies had not entered the church, so there had to be some truth to whatever was behind the door was protecting them.

Sarah walked up beside her, keeping the M16 she had taken from Cecil, pointed toward the people along the wall. A blue light filled the opening, frame to frame like a drape. "That light is just like the force field on the alien ship."

"Force field?" Clare said, pulling the door further open. "Is it safe to go through it and inside the room?"

"I don't know," Sarah said. "It acts as a barrier, keeping areas separated. On the spaceship, it was used on doors, like the ones in the airlock."

Clare looked through the transparent film covering the door entry. In the room, she saw a circular tube of blue light. "What's that?"

Sarah looked inside. "I don't know. Is it a transporter?"

Clare turned toward the Cartwrights, still facing the wall. "What is this room? What is that tube of light?"

The Cartwrights did not answer.

"What happened to you two?" Sarah said, feeling somewhat sad. The Cartwrights were not in their right mind, and she knew this was not their normal behavior. But on the other hand, the Cartwrights spoke of their so-called religion as if they were truly faking kindness and did indeed consider Sarah and the rest of them infidels, to say the least. "Both of you, and you, too, Cecil, were level headed and kind. Now you're . . . completely different. All I can say is I hope you can see what that vaccine has done to you."

"Are the doses new?" Clare asked, speaking toward The Community members. "Freshly made by aliens? If so, maybe they changed something, made them more potent, or made them so that the side effects are accelerated. The aliens can't be trusted."

"They are protecting us right now," Mrs. Cartwright said with a muted voice. "They are keeping us safe."

"Then explain this," Clare said. "Why are they letting you starve? The only thing they've given you is the stuff in those needles . . . a toxin."

"Where are Jibber and Miss Foo?" Georgie asked, holding his sword. "What did you do with them?"

No one answered him.

Clare looked deeper inside the room. A pedestal with a panel of lit symbols was next to the tube, and then she noticed something lying on the floor next to it. She studied it a moment. "Sarah, what's that on the floor?"

Sarah looked to where Clare was pointing. "It looks like a dog biscuit. They must've lured the dogs inside the room."

Cecil held back a laugh. "You have the dumbest and most troublesome mutts. We sent them through the transporter."

Sarah looked back inside the room. "Where does the transporter go? To the spaceship?"

"You got it," Cecil said, holding back a laugh.

Willis held back tears. "Mom, did they feed them to the bioship?"

Soon the whole group of preppers was laughing.

Clare was furious. "Okay, that settles it. I've learned that the aliens can't be trusted, and you people can't be trusted. You are all going to the jail. There's room for all of you in that dirty and dark hovel."

They all abruptly stopped laughing.

"No, we won't leave here," Cecil said, defiantly stiffening his body posture.

"Move it, now," Clare demanded. But they would not budge.

"We're not going anywhere," Mrs. Cartwright said, seemingly unruffled by Clare's demand. "You won't shoot us."

"Maybe I should," Clare said. "I don't want to shoot you, but I will. You can trust me on that."

"I don't think you will," Mrs. Cartwright said, turning her head to look at them. "Neither will Sarah."

Clare aimed her .44 Magnum revolver toward them, but not directly at them. She pulled the trigger, but the gun did not fire. She tried again, but nothing happened.

The Community turned around and laughed.

"It was fun playing along," Mrs. Cartwright said with a smirk. She placed a hand gently over her stomach and sighed with relief. "None of your weapons work. I wasn't sure if that was the case since no one has ever fired a gun inside the church before. But now I know you're helpless."

Georgie stepped up, holding his sword in a low open stance. He had the straight-bladed sword angled slightly downward and to the right. "I can use this and I'm not afraid."

"You're just a wee lad," Cecil said, crossing his arms. "You don't have it in yourself to harm us."

Unworried by Georgie's threat, one of The Community members looked out a window. "The zombies have us surrounded and something is falling from the sky like snow."

Soon all The Community members clamored for a window. They gasped when they saw the zombies waiting outside for them.

"Dawn," Clare said, still gripping her revolver. "See if you can tell how many zombies are outside."

Dawn walked to a window and looked out into the darkness and at the zombies, illuminated by the glowing blue dome covering the church. She gasped. "There's at least a dozen that I see and look to be outside the dome and are standing side-by-side. It looks like they are circling the church."

Sarah whispered to Clare, "What are we going to do?"

Even though Clare's revolver would not work, she still kept it pointed at The Community members. She whispered to Sarah, "We could leave the church, but we'd be overtaken by the zombies; we don't have enough ammunition to fight our way through them. If we turn off the device keeping our weapons from working, it may lower the energy shield and the zombies will come inside. We can wait inside until the guys get back, but that could be a couple days."

Sarah studied the door to the sacristy. She did not see a symbol used for a lock like the doors on the spaceship so she would not have to use her hand to enable them to walk through the field. Looking deeper into the room, she noticed that the symbols on the pedestal panel looked similar to the ones in the spaceship's room with the black boxes. She was about to tell Clare about the symbols when The Community members ran past them, through the door's force field, and into the transporter tube, where they disappeared.

Clare and Sarah stepped back to allow them to escape to the spaceship. Mrs. Cartwright was in line. She stopped and looked at Sarah.

"Sarah, dear, I'm sorry for deceiving you, but we must do what the heavenly brothers say so that we are protected."

Sarah looked at her big protruding eyeballs. They had grown in the last couple of days. The eyes were now similar to big-eyed bugs. She was shocked to see a nub between Mrs. Cartwrights nose and mouth. Was Mrs. Cartwright growing a piercing, sucking mouthpart, like those used by bugs to stab and suck juices from their prey? Sarah felt sorry for Mrs. Cartwright, the aliens had taken advantage of The Community and now it was too late to help them.

"I'm sorry for your predicament," Sarah said, meaning every word. She looked away.

Mrs. Cartwright smiled, then turned and followed the others into the transporter tube.

When the last person disappeared into the tube the blue light, coming in through the windows, flickered then when out.

"What just happened?" Georgie asked, looking around the darkened and empty church.

Dawn ran back to the window. "The dome went out and the zombies are walking toward us."

Within seconds, there was pounding on the church's front door and walls.

"The dome is gone, we're not protected anymore," Sarah said. The panic that was subsiding had now returned.

"At least are guns will work now," Clare said, pointing the revolver toward the door.

"We need to go into the transporter," Georgie said, walking toward the room. "We need to find Jibber and Miss Foo."

Then the front door opened and crazed zombies, soaking wet and walking awkwardly fast, entered the church, heading straight toward them.

Clare shot one walking dead square in the forehead, it stumbled backward. "Looks like we're going through the transporter. Any objection, Sarah?"

"No," she said, pointing the wand at the quickly approaching zombies. A gold beam shot out toward the walking corpses, stunning them, confusing them, making them stop. "Don't go in the transporter until I look at the panel."

"Hurry up," Clare said, directing the kids to follow Sarah into the sacristy.

Sarah looked at the symbols on the panel. They were indeed like the ones she and Max were deciphering in the black box room on the ship.

"They're moving," Clare said, stepping through the transparent blue barrier and into the room with the others, closing the wood door behind her. "I don't think this is going to keep them out long."

Sarah was so panicked she did not know what symbol to push, if any. If only she knew where the preppers had gone, yet she did not want to keep company with people who were so willing to sacrifice them. On the other hand, she did not want them to end up in a box or fed to the ship. She did not know much about hieroglyphs but based on what Max had taught her, the one that was currently lit was the symbol Amenta, it represented the Underworld or Land of the Dead. She did not want to go there.

As the zombies pounded on the sacristy door like possessed demons, she pressed the symbol Ankh on the pedestal, representing eternal life. It lit up, making a soft tone. "Clare, I'm as ready as I'll ever be. I'll go first."

"Okay," Clare said, keeping her gun pointed toward the door as she backed toward the transporter.

"You kids follow right behind me," Sarah said, and then she stepped into the tube of blue light and disappeared.

Willis, Georgie, and Dawn were right behind her. Then Clare stepped into the tube.

EIGHTEEN

Jack put the motorhome into drive. The wheels spun, eventually getting traction, propelling them forward and down the road. "Is Ray following us or is he stuck, too?"

Max looked at the side mirror. "Looks like he's following us. I think the semi has enough power to break free from the bloody grip of that . . . monster moss."

Jack laughed. "How about vile vines or wicked weeds?"

"Barbarian bryophytes," the professor blurted out.

"Barbarian what?" Jack said, keeping both hands on the steering wheel.

"Bryophytes are mosses, liverworts, and hornworts," the professor said.

"Sounds like something from Harry Potter," Jack said, keeping his eyes on the moss-covered road. It was as though he was driving on a pink strip of carpet.

"Pay attention to the road, Jack," Max grumbled. "If your brain gets overworked thinking about scientific classification, we'll end up in the ditch."

Jack glanced at Max and then back to the road. "Thanks for the vote of support for my mental capabilities."

Max turned his attention from the rhythmical beating of the windshield wipers and spores smearing over the glass, to the map on his lap. "Take a left at the next road."

The motorhome's headlights had difficulty penetrating the blizzard of spores as they approached an intersection. A layer of moss, just like the moss colonizing the trees, obscured the road sign.

"I can't read the sign," Jack said, slowing down, but not stopping for fear of being stuck again.

The professor got up from the recliner he had claimed for his own—but then, no one wanted to sit in it anyway, ever since he bled all over it when he was changing into a zombie—and then looked at the sign. Then he looked at the totally covered forest, where the trees were breaking down. "Moss typically acts as an epiphyte, but this alien moss is a parasite, feeding off the trees and other plants."

"Epi . . . what?" Jack said, keeping the motorhome creeping forward.

"Epiphytes are plants that grow on other plants but does not harm them," the professor said, scanning the darkened landscape. "They basically just use the plants for physical support. But just like my experiments were showing, this moss is destructive and looks like it has accelerated its ability to destroy the planet's vegetation."

"That has to be the road," Max said, pointing to the left.

"I'm turning down it," Jack said, turning the steering wheel. The motorhome struggled as its wheels spun, barely making progress. "Shit, the moss is trying to stop us."

"Power on through it," Tony said, with a nasally voice. He was so congested he was beginning to wheeze. "Did anyone get an antihistamine when you were at the store?"

"There are some in the compound's hospital," the professor said. "I'll get them for you when we get back."

"I feel like I'm driving through peanut butter," Jack said, keeping steady pressure on the accelerator. "Oh wait, I mean monster moss."

Max was about to tell Jack to keep his eyes on the road and not steer them into a ditch, when he looked down at his pant legs to brush off what he thought was a bug crawling up his khaki janitor style pants. He shrieked as he jumped out of the passenger seat.

"What? What's going on?" Jack asked, startled. He almost lost control of the motorhome, swerving to keep from going into the ditch that Max was trying to get him to avoid. He turned to look at Max, who was staring at his legs. "What the hell?"

"Don't move," the professor said. He stood up and took the flashlight from the console. He turned on the bright light and leaned forward to get a closer look at the moss growing on Max's legs, encasing them like the trees and street signs outside.

Max looked down at the red veins coating his lower body. He began ripping the rigid cartilage from his legs. The veins started to bleed as he dropped the crusty material and elastic tendons to the floor where it began to squirm and reach for Max's foot.

"That's just like an exoskeleton," the professor said. He reached into his camouflage jacket for a pen and began poking at the shell. "The alien moss has evolved into an organism that is set on preservation."

Max kicked the squirming mass into the stairwell. "That shit was trying to coat me a shell like a cockroach."

"Look at those sucking tubes," the professor said, still examining the alien life form with his pen. "I wouldn't be surprised if it tried to penetrate your skin and attach apodemes to your muscles."

"And control me like a marionette?" Max said, wiping his hands with the remaining hand wipes.

"Is it half plant and half animal?" Father asked, staying in the galley. "Is that possible?"

"Elysia chlorotica, also known as green sea slugs are animals that are able to use chlorophyll to capture energy from the sun," the professor said. "That snail even looks like a leaf."

"I bet the green sea slug isn't a man-eater like that monster moss," Tony said as he sat up and moved to the far side of the sofa, away from all the action.

"This alien moss isn't green and doesn't seem to like bright light in its advanced stage," the professor said, watching the vine crawl away as he shined the light on it. "I wonder what it will do when the sun rises in the morning."

The professor tossed his pen into the stairwell with the vines as the motorhome continued to rumble down the road.

"You'd better check Jack," Tony said. "He was outside with Max."

They looked at Jack, who was concentrating on the road. The professor shined the light at Jack's legs. They gasped when they saw that the same type of exoskeleton had attached itself to his lower body.

"Jack," Max said, as calmly as he could. "Don't panic, but . . ."

Jack turned his focus from the road and looked down at his lap. He slammed on the brakes, bringing the motorhome to a stop as he jumped out of the seat.

"What the frickin' hell," he said as he began ripping the stretchy blood vessels and the friable coating from his legs. Max got in the driver's seat and punched the gas. The motorhome spun its wheels.

"We're stuck," Max shouted, having lost the last speck of calmness he was trying to exert.

Jack opened the motorhome's door and shoved the vines, vessels, and bony material out the door. When the last of the organism was out of the motorhome, he slammed the door shut, and went to Max, who had the gas pedal floored. "Move, let me do it."

Max got out of the seat and looked at his blood stained pants. "Shit, now I'm going to have to put on the rest of that morbid Goth outfit."

Father handed Max a pair of black denim jeans with leather on the knees and a zipper fly. He shrugged. "At least they don't have blood on them."

Max groaned as he took off his bloody khakis and tossed them in the stepwell. He put on the slim-fitting pants, using the skull and dagger pull tab on the zipper, and put his magnetic alien boots back on. "Don't anyone laugh."

The professor began laughing. "Max, I think you found your style."

"I wish I could see," Tony said.

"Hey, you guys," Jack said, tensed. "I'm glad you're having a good time put we're not going anyplace."

"We can't go back out there and cut the tires free," Max said, testing the jeans by bending at the knee. "Or that stuff is going to have us looking like some freaky cartoon character."

"Maybe it acts like a body suit and gives the wearer inhuman strength," Jack said, still trying to get the motorhome to move.

"I don't think I like the idea of those tendrils puncturing my skin and attaching themselves to my muscles," Max said, returning to the passenger seat. "But you can do it if you like."

Then there was a bump from behind.

"What was that?" Tony asked.

Jack looked in the side mirror. "It's Ray, he's trying to push us with the truck."

Ray kept the nose of the cab touching the back of the motorhome as Jack pressed his foot on the accelerator until it was broken free.

"Stay on the road, Jack," Max said, sitting back in the passenger seat.

"I'm trying, but this tuna boat wants to slide off the crown of the road," Jack said as perspiration dripped down his face.

"Slow down," Max said, reaching for the dashboard for support. "There's a curve ahead."

"Oh shit," Jack said. "Brace yourself."

Jack took his foot off the gas pedal but did not put it on the brake, knowing that it would likely cause the motorhome to slide, something it was probably going to do anyway once he turned the steering wheel.

Max fastened his seatbelt just before the side of the motorhome slammed into the steel box beam guardrail, preventing them from rolling, end over end, down an embankment into a river filled with floating moss covered debris.

The motorhome's fiberglass sidewalls scraped along the guardrail, creating an unnerving screech as Jack held the steering wheel tight, and then yanked it back the other way, keeping them from spinning out of control. Cans of baked beans and soup rolled around the floor while everything unsecured flew toward the impact wall.

Jack gave the motorhome gas, straightened out its path and continued driving down the road. "We'd better be almost to the compound because I can't take much more of this."

"Everything looks so foreign with that terraforming shit all over the place. But I think that river is the one that feeds Lake 66, at least according to the map, so it should be straight ahead," Max said.

"Is the trailer still attached?" Tony asked.

Max looked out the side mirror. "The fender's dangling, otherwise we still have it."

"I don't want to worry anyone," Father said, "but how are we going to be able to leave the RV. Those plant-animal things will start climbing up our legs."

"No plastic bags on our feet," Jack said. "We tried that before and it's clumsy as hell."

"That won't work anyway, Jack," Max said. "Those things will crawl right up it."

"We need to kill it," Tony said.

"We need to at least repel it," the professor said, still grasping the recliner's armrests.

"With what?" Jack asked. "It grows on everything."

"Slow down," Max said, annoyed as he stomped the floor. "There's my Mustang and it's covered with that crap."

Jack pulled the motorhome around Max's car so that he and Ray had enough room to pull the LNG tanker next to Pegasus for refueling. He stopped driving when he was facing back down the road.

"The compound looks dead, there aren't any lights," Max said, looking at the dark community behind the wall. "I don't see any signs of life. It's like a blanket, weaved with blood vessels and vines, was laid over everything."

Jack rolled down his driver's window and shouted to Ray. "Don't get out yet until we figure out what to do about the moss."

Ray nodded and rolled his window back up.

"We know it doesn't like bright beams of light shined on it," Max said. "But we don't have enough flashlights to make it safe to be outside for any length of time."

"Moss doesn't like chemicals like herbicides, ferrous sulfate, ammonium sulfate, and copper sulfate," the professor said. "But we don't have any of that."

"We do have a tanker full of methane," Max said, unfastening his seatbelt. "But that's for our getaway."

"There are propane tanks on the trailer," Jack added, turning to face the others.

"There's a fire extinguisher on the wall, maybe that could work, too," Father said, pointing toward the door.

"How are we going to find the others inside the compound?" Max asked, rubbing his moist palms over his new jeans.

"Should we blow the horn to get Sarah and Clare's attention?" Father asked.

"Yeah, that's a good idea," Jack said. "But I need to make sure it's safe to even go outside."

"If propane works against that monster moss," Jack said, "we'll need a propane hose and a nozzle and I don't think we have anything like that."

"We could turn on the spotlights that the preppers have in their tower," Tony said. "If there's still power."

"Is there anything the organism won't attach itself to?" the professor asked. "We know it attaches to people, vehicles, trees, bushes, roads, and the ground."

"I can't think of anything it doesn't grow on," Jack said.

"I found another fire extinguisher," Father said, unhooking it from the galley wall.

Max opened the glove box and took out the vehicle owner's manual. "According to this, there should also be an extinguisher in the bedroom and another in the storage compartment under the coach."

"I'll climb over the food and see if I can find the one in the bedroom," Father said, looking at heaps of food in the bedroom and scattered all over the floor.

"Before you climb over that mess, we need to see if the fire extinguishers even work on it," Jack said, walking toward the door. "Can you see yet, Tony?"

"Barely," Tony said, blowing his nose.

Jack took the extinguisher by the door and pulled the pin in the handle. "Okay, I'm opening the door."

Jack opened the door while Max shined the flashlight at the moss. He aimed the nozzle at the vines on the ground. He squeezed the lever and did a short sweep. "It's shrinking and backing away."

"I think fire extinguishers last less than a minute, though," the professor said, trying to reposition his body in a chair that was a size too small.

"Well, then why are we trying this? It's a waste of time," Jack said, closing the door.

"Your alien pistol, Jack," Tony said. "Try that."

"Of course, why didn't I think of that?" Jack said, taking it from the back waistband of his blood-stained jeans. He looked at what he and Tony had previously determined to be an intensity adjuster when they were target practicing with it. He set it to a low level since he would be firing so close to the motorhome; he did not want to blow them up.

He opened the door again and shot a beam of laser light along the ground, twenty feet from the motorhome. The moss stopped moving as it began smoking. "It appears I stunned it and burned it." He turned around and picked up a can of peas. "Who picked these? Are you trying to piss off the preppers?" He tossed it into the fried moss. It did not move.

"I think it worked," Max said, peering through the door.

"Stay here," Jack said, cutting a path to the tanker truck. "I'm going to help Ray get Pegasus fueled and ready for launch, and then we'll go into the compound. I want to be sure our escape vessel is ready to go just in case we're running for our lives."

"Sounds familiar," Max said, closing the door behind him.

NINETEEN

The minute Sarah, Clare, and the kids stepped out of the transporter; humans with alien handguns surrounded them. They froze, trying to make sense of where they were.

Then Sarah saw Randy, standing with a smirk in the circle of human workers. "Randy?"

"I'm surprised you decided to come back to Mars," Randy said, amused. Then his grin turned to a frown. "Drop your weapons."

Sarah tried to sneak the alien wand into her purse, but Randy noticed.

"Even the wand," Randy said, motioning for a worker to approach her.

Sarah sat the wand and the M16 on the floor. Clare did the same with her .44 Magnum revolver.

Randy looked at Georgie. "The sword, too."

Now they were defenseless.

"Randy," Sarah said, wanting to reason with him. "You know us."

Randy snorted. "Yeah, I remember you and Jack." He pulled up the sleeve of his green overalls. "I remember you and Jack putting this prisoner band on me. Now I'm trapped here."

"You've been here?" Clare whispered to Sarah. "Where exactly are we?"

"It appears we're in the platform on Mars, inside the volcano, Olympus Mons."

Randy motioned for them to begin walking down the corridor as the circle of men followed. "Very good, Sarah. Where is your boyfriend, Jack?"

Sarah did not say anything as she kept walking to what appeared to be jail cells. One of the workers opened a door and the five of them walked inside.

The worker closed and locked the door as Randy stood in the corridor in front of the jail bars. "You didn't answer me, where's Jack?"

Sarah shrugged. "I don't know; he went to get food for The Community." Sarah looked around. "Where are they?"

"Where are who?" Randy asked. "The members of The Community?"

"Yeah, you haven't seen them?" Sarah asked, acting concerned.

He began walking away with the other men. "Nope, I haven't seen them." He stopped and turned back toward them. A big wide grin formed on his bony face. "Because they're in the hoosegow." He continued walking.

"What's a hoosegow?" Georgie asked, touching his empty scabbard.

"It's a prison," Sarah said. "Probably the black boxes."

"Good thing you pressed a different button," Georgie said. "I don't want to go back into one of those things."

"Yeah, I suppose," Sarah said, looking around the jail cell. "We're still prisoners, though."

"We have to find Jibber and Miss Foo," Willis said. He walked up to the bars, trying to see down both sides of the long hallway.

"We need to get back to the transporter," Clare said. "Hopefully, the zombies have given up on us and . . ." She was interrupted by the sound of zombie moans and a buzzing sound. "Sounds like the zombies followed us through the transporter and the guards are stopping them."

Sarah went to the jail bars and looked down the hall toward the transporter. "You're right; they're dropping like flies."

"Getting out of here is not going to be easy," Clare said, feeling her empty holster. "They took all our weapons. I'm going to need to think about this."

"Maybe I can reason with Randy," Sarah said, turning toward Clare. "If he and the other workers have not been taking that altered vaccine like the preppers at the compound, he should have some sense left in his head."

"They don't look like they've been taking the new vaccine," Dawn said, standing next to her mom. "They're not growing a long tubular mouth for sucking."

Willis laughed. "Yeah, they looked like they were growing a proboscis. In science class, we learned that bugs use it to feed on plant fluid. Assassin bugs use it to poke into their prey and suck their blood."

"That's gross," Dawn said, covering her mouth with her hand.

"Why would they turn them into that?" Georgie asked, leaning against the bars.

"Maybe they're creating a superior warrior," Clare said. She sat down and leaned against the cell's back wall. "Tony told me the government is trying to create super soldiers that are part human and part chimpanzee. That type of soldier would be powerful on Earth but maybe not on other planets. Maybe the cross between humans and assassin bugs can better tolerate space and the different types of environments on planets."

"A few months ago I would have said you were crazy," Sarah said, sitting down. "But now, not so much."

"They would also make good soldiers because they're good at hunting and are natural born killers," Willis said. He looked at Dawn to see if she liked his intelligent remarks. "Soon they'll probably be sprouting antennae."

Georgie and Dawn laughed.

"Let me see if I'm getting all this straight," Sarah said, stretching her legs. "The zombies kill humans and then die, which leaves Earth for the aliens. But before they die they turn into cocoons where a tornen grows inside them."

"And the aliens love to eat those tornen," Willis said. He laughed.

"But if the tornen are left to hatch, they hunt humans," Sarah continued. "And now we have preppers, the people in The Community, who voluntarily allowed themselves to be injected, with what they thought was a vaccine to keep them from changing into zombies. But instead, it is turning them into some type of super soldier."

"Don't forget the aliens," Clare said, removing her camo cap. "There are the half-breed aliens and the reptilians and they are terraforming Earth so they can live on it." She ran her fingers through her hair and then put

111

her cap back on. "I've seen Rausuca and a couple other hybrid aliens, but I haven't seen a reptilian, yet."

"You don't want to see the reptilians," Sarah said. "I think those lizard people are eviler than the hybrids. And they're here on Mars."

"So I've heard," Clare said. "Tony said they're even inside the earth . . . underground."

"That was one of the symbols on the panel by the transporter," Sarah said. "That was where the preppers went when they ran into the transporter—they went to the Underworld, also called the Land of the Dead."

"I guess some of Tony's crackpot ideas aren't too far off." Clare giggled as she leaned her head back against the hard wall.

"Us humans are nothing more than bugs to be squashed," Sarah said. "If they can't use us for breeding or as killing machines, they'll simply dispose of us."

"Yeah, by feeding us to their bioships," Willis said, noticing Dawn was smiling at him.

"I don't see how we can possibly win against them," Sarah said.

"Well, don't lose hope," Clare said, closing her eyes. "There has to be a way."

TWENTY

Ray had opened the door to the truck cab before Jack jumped up on the step.

"I was wondering how we were going to fight our way through those weird plants," Ray said, looking at the compound. "But sad to say, it doesn't seem like anyone's . . ."

Jack hung his head a moment and nodded. "Yeah, I know. It doesn't look good, but I was thinking I'll clear a path to Pegasus so that you can begin refueling and then I'll head inside the compound to find the others."

"Who's going with you?" Ray asked, raising his eyebrows. "You're not going alone, are you?"

"Tony still can't see so he'll have to stay behind," Jack said, still gripping the grab bar. "So that leaves the professor with his pistol and probably Max with Tony's rifle. Father can watch over Tony."

"Don't take long because I have a feeling those plants won't stay motionless forever," Ray said, picking up a flashlight and the M16 lying in the seat beside him. "When I'm done here I'll check on Tony and Father and probably bring them back here so we're ready to launch."

Jack agreed. He jumped off the cab's step and cleared a path around the tanker and Pegasus. He helped Ray get setup to begin pumping the methane into the spacecraft. They pulled the veiny vines off Pegasus and threw them on the ground where Jack promptly zapped them.

Ray opened the hatch and went inside the capsule. "It looks fine in here."

"Blow your horn if you get into any trouble," Jack said.

"Don't worry," Ray said as he began hooking up the LNG hose to Pegasus.

Jack walked back to the motorhome and walked inside. He looked at Tony. "Can you see, yet? The spores have stopped coming down, at least for now."

"Nope, not yet," Tony said, wiping his eyes.

"I was thinking that Father could stay with you, Tony, and the professor and Max can come with me." Jack looked at the others. "Professor, you have your pistol and Max you can use Tony's rifle."

"That leaves us with no weapons," Tony said. "But we'll manage."

"Ray has an M16 and when he's done refueling Pegasus he'll join you guys," Jack said. He looked at the professor who was sliding his hefty body forward in the recliner. Then he looked at Max seated in the passenger seat. His unshaven jaw quivered, but he did not protest the plan. "Let's go while we can."

The three men had flashlights and their weapons raised as they walked out of the motorhome. The sound of the cargo transfer pump chattered from the back of the tanker.

Jack shined his flashlight toward the noise. He saw Ray with the M16 hanging across his body while he was busy connecting a hose and checking valves and gauges.

Ray noticed the others leaving the motorhome; he gave them a thumbs-up.

Jack nodded and began clearing a path through several inches of spores and hybrid moss. As they got closer, Jack noticed the main gate was partially opened. He walked toward it with the professor behind him and Max bringing up the rear.

"I wonder why the gate is open," the professor said. "Did they all leave the compound?"

"I don't know where they would go," Jack said, moving the beam of his light around the door. "They'd be better off staying behind the walls."

They approached the open gate. Jack shined the light inside the courtyard before walking inside. All he saw was buildings covered with the vines; some of the buildings appeared to be collapsing under the weight of the plants or from being digested.

Max looked over at the shed housing his portable eighteen inch Dobsonian telescope. The roof had collapsed on it and vines had climbed around and encased the tube and all its parts. He looked up at the dark sky where a few of the brighter stars managed to penetrate the haze. "Damn. We were gone only a day and my Dobsonian, Mustang, and the compound have been destroyed. I guess the preppers won't need our food."

"Screw the physical things, I just hope Sarah and the others are safe," Jack said, cutting a path toward the Cartwrights. The alien light beam flashed like a disco light show as it burned through the vines, which were moving around them like earthworms. Then he stopped. "What the hell."

The professor shined his flashlight where Jack was looking. "Now we know why they were leaving the compound."

The three of them shined their lights on zombies entwined by the vines. The fleshy tubes appeared to be feeding on the dead and decaying people.

Jack scanned the area and saw several more zombies captured by the vines, especially by the church. "Are they all zombies or are some of them members of The Community?"

The professor shined his light around at the spectacle. "Hard to tell, but from the looks of these people I'd say they have been decomposing for quite some time, so I'd say they are zombies."

"Where are the preppers," Jack said. Then he shouted, "Sarah, Clare, kids, where are you? It's Jack."

There was no answer. All they heard was the tanker pump.

"Jack," the professor said, shining his light toward the church. "I think that when we're done looking in the Cartwrights that we should check out the church; there seems to be a cluster of zombies around it."

Jack nodded and continued cutting a path to the Cartwrights porch. He ripped the bloody veins from the door and opened it. "Sarah, are you in here?" No answer.

The three walked inside and into the kitchen. Jack shined his light at the dining room table. "Shit, empty syringes. These community people just don't know when to stop."

The professor picked up a syringe and inspected it. "This looks like the BW vaccine and there are several used ones. I hope they didn't force . . ."

"We can't think that way, Professor," Jack said, angry. "We're finding them and they'll be okay. Sarah and the others would not allow themselves to be injected without a fight."

They continued into the living room. "Let's check upstairs."

They walked up the steps to the hallway leading to the bedrooms. Jack almost fell when he slipped on a slimy substance. He shined his light to the ceiling and saw a sap like substance dripping from the plaster. A drop fell on his hand, burning it. "Damn it." He wiped the juice on his pant leg.

"It's probably a digestive substance and it's digesting the house . . . and us if we stay in here."

"Sarah, anyone," Jack shouted. Still no response.

"I suggest we get to the church while we can," the professor said, as digestives juices dripped around them.

They walked back downstairs and out the front door. Jack cut a path toward the church, zigzagging around the trapped zombies.

"Jack. That zombie is moving." Max's voice trembled. He shined his light toward a zombie covered in vines. The veins were penetrating an eye and had entered the mouth and nostrils of the rotting flesh on the zombie's skull.

"Let's keep moving," Jack said, clearing a path to the broken church door. He shined the light down the aisle of the nave toward the sanctuary. He stepped inside, shining the light from pew to pew. "Sarah, are you in here?"

"Look at the sacristy door," the professor said, shining his light toward the front of the church and the pale blue light radiating through the fractured door.

"That light looks familiar," Max said, staying closer to Jack than to the professor.

Jack stepped up toward the altar and saw three chairs with ropes lying beside them. "Looks like they had someone tied up."

Max looked at the syringes and chalice. "And it seems they had some weird service going on."

The professor walked toward the sacristy door. "There's a tube of light in there. Have you two seen that before?"

"The light is the same color as the one on the spaceship," Max said, looking at the transparent blue cylinder of light.

The three stood in front of the sacristy door. Jack stepped inside and looked at the pedestal and the lit emblems. "Max is right, this is definitely alien shit, but I've never seen that tube of blue light before."

The professor walked up next to Jack and the pedestal. "Could it be a type of transporter? A way to get on the spaceship?"

Max looked at the symbols. "I recognize some of these symbols. These here probably go to the black boxes, but I don't know where the other ones take you."

"Does that mean they transported up to the spaceship and are now prisoners?" Jack asked. The muscles in his neck and jaw were tightening.

Max pointed at the symbol outlined with a blue light. "This appears to be the last button pushed and it isn't one of the ones for the black boxes, at least that I know of."

"Sarah," Jack shouted. His effort was futile.

"If this is indeed a transporter," the professor said, "it's possible they stepped inside. I'm thinking that it is a likely scenario because of all the zombies surrounding the church and the broken doors."

"There are no zombies in the church," Jack said, shining his light around the room filled with blue light.

"They probably followed them into the transporter," the professor said.

"Shit, now what do we do?" Jack said, tensing and then releasing his shoulders.

"If we go into the transporter, we may not come back," Max said, studying the panel. "Especially if we get caged."

Jack knelt down and picked up the dog biscuit lying on the floor. "They went through it," Jack said holding up the biscuit. "If the dogs were coaxed into it, the kids, Sarah, and Clare would have gone through it to rescue them . . . zombies or not."

Max shook his head. "It could also have taken them directly to the bioship's stomach."

"I'll take my chances," Jack said. He looked at the professor and Max. "You don't have to go with me, you can stay here with Ray and Tony."

Max grumbled. "I have to go with you, Jack. You're too dense to figure out what the symbols mean. You'll get everyone killed."

Jack smiled. "You have a way with words, Max."

"I don't feel right us splitting up," the professor said. "You could end up someplace different than the others and then we'll have three groups of people to get back together."

"Believe it or not," Max said, frowning. "Jack is right. It makes more sense for you to stay here because Ray may need your help operating Pegasus. Tony is useless until that allergy clears up. Father can help, but he's not a scientist."

"I think you're getting used to me, Maxy Boy," Jack said, displaying a broad grin.

Max began grinding his teeth. "Don't push it, Jack, or you'll be going into that light beam all by yourself."

"Okay," the professor said, changing the subject. "Let's get to it before these zoophytes start making the paths impassable."

"I'd like to say don't wait for us if we're taking too long," Jack said, turning toward the tube of transparent blue light. "But I would like to get the hell away from here, too."

"We'll wait as long as we can," the professor said, turning toward the door. "Just make sure getting back here with the others is your top priority."

"What else would be my top priority?" Jack asked. He turned toward Max. "Are you ready?"

"As ready as I'll ever be," Max said, following Jack into the transporter.

TWENTY-ONE

No sooner had they stepped into the transporter when Jack and Max found themselves inside a physical structure. They did not speak as they stepped off the raised floor, rumbling under their feet. It seemed that the structure was going to topple on top of them. Then an alarm began to sound.

"This way," Jack said, running the opposite direction of the shouts and footsteps of people approaching.

Five corridors surrounded the center expanse, like the spokes of a wheel. They ran down one of the spokes. The only place they saw to hide was behind one of the steel I-beams used for structural support. They pressed their backs against the wall so that when the workers looked down the corridor, they would not be seen. They heard them talking and wondering if it was a malfunction because of the spaceship landing, causing an unusual shaking to the platform. Soon the voices faded and went back from where they had come.

Jack poked his head slowly around the steel frame; the workers had gone. "That was close," he whispered.

"We could be in the platform on Mars," Max said, running his hand along the metal wall. "But it's unusual that they use I-beams like on Earth. Especially since the alien spacecraft had walls similar to snake skin."

"I think you're right," Jack said. "It could be that since human workers are housed here, they made the structure out of things they were familiar with and could repair."

"I can't believe we're back on Mars," Max grumbled.

"I'm not happy about it either," Jack said, holding the alien handgun. "Especially since the workers have the ability to block this gun." He looked at Max holding Tony's rifle at his side. "I'm tempted to trade weapons, but as far as I know, they're not aware we're here."

Jack looked up and down the corridor. "Now we have to find the others. Any idea where we should go?"

"We don't want to go to their control room," Max said, pointing down the corridor from where they had come. "They probably are holding the others someplace . . . hopefully not in a black box."

"Let's check this corridor first," Jack said, walking toward the end. The floor was shiny and the corridor was wide. Then a whirring sound grew louder. "Quick, against the wall."

They watched as a golf-cart type vehicle sped past the end of the corridor, driving around what appeared to be a ring-shaped outer hallway, circling the inside of the round structure. Then the building rumbled again.

"That was either a minor earthquake or they're still having trouble with the spaceship on top of us," Max said, looking toward the tall ceiling.

When they reached the end of the long corridor, they could see through the windows to the darkened tropical environment outside. Palm-like plants, conifers, and ferns were lit by the glow cast from the blue dome encompassing the platform.

"Yep, we're definitely back on Mars and inside Olympus Mons," Max said, shaking his head. "They must pump extra oxygen into the building because I'm not having any difficulty breathing."

"Look," Jack said, walking up to a box on the wall. "What are these?"

Max walked up to the wall box filled with Bluetooth like devices, each with a thin line, measuring a few inches, protruding from the side like a microphone on a headset. A sign with O2 written on it was directly above it. "I bet they're a type of breathing apparatus. They must hook over the ear and then the tube is placed next to the nose for breathing in oxygen."

"Randy never said anything about these," Jack said, taking one and placing it over his ear.

"He probably didn't want you having any advantage over him," Max said, doing the same.

"Now we have to find the others," Jack said. "They could be locked in the platform, on the spaceship, or in the corral with a slew of other creatures."

"At least I don't see hieroglyphs all over the place," Max said, looking around.

"Like that room," Jack said, pointing across the corridor. "It says locker room."

Max squinted at Jack. "So do you have to go to the bathroom, Jack?"

Jack smiled. "Come to think of it, maybe I do."

They looked both ways down the vacant corridor before walking across to the door. They looked in through the small window; there was no one inside.

"They're probably all busy helping to unload the spaceship," Max said. "If we're going to do things inside this platform, we need to do it before their job is completed."

Jack opened the door and they walked inside. There were rows of lockers and a bathroom at the far end of the room. He tested the lockers until he found an unlocked one. It was empty. He walked toward the toilet and an open closet. "Jackpot."

Max walked up next to Jack, who was pulling out and looking at green coveralls and hard hats. "Are you thinking what I'm thinking?"

Jack nodded. "I think we just became human workers on the planet Mars."

They donned the coveralls and hard hats and then looked at themselves in the bathroom mirror.

"Now all we have to do is act like assholes and we'll fit right in," Jack said, grinning as he looked over at Max.

"That shouldn't be hard for you to do," Max said, feeling his stubby beard.

"Hey, I resent that," Jack said, standing up straight. "I'm a pretty nice guy."

They were walking from the bathroom, with their weapons in hand, when they heard the locker room door open and two people talking. They both turned and pretended to be getting inside a locker as the two men walked past them. Then one of the men stopped and turned toward them.

"You two had better hurry up," one of the human workers said.

Adrenaline surged through Jack's body as he pretended to be a worker trying to get into his locker. He kept his head down as he worked at the combination lock. "We're on our way."

Jack and Max were about to turn to leave when the other worker said. "Hey, where are your ID tags?"

They were had. Jack had to think of something to say that sounded realistic. "That's why we came in here. Those damned infidels grabbed them from us when we were putting them in the corral."

Both men gave Jack a long stare.

"You don't say," one of the workers said. He was less deformed than the ones on Earth.

Jack knew they did not believe his line of bullshit. His trigger finger twitched, as he debated whether to shoot the workers before they had a chance to block his alien handgun and keep it from working. Of course, Max had Tony's rifle, but that would be loud, and besides, Max probably would not use it. He smiled and nodded as he began to turn. From the corner of his eye, he saw them resting their hands on their guns, holstered at the hip. Without even thinking, letting his instincts drive his moves, he raised his handgun and pulled the trigger. Nothing happened. Shit, it is blocked. Again, with little thought he charged them, hitting the first one in the jaw with his fist. He reached for the second one's handgun as the first one stumbled back, apparently surprised by the quick attack. While Jack tried to take the alien gun from the second one, he shouted, "Max, help me."

Max raised the rifle. His hands and voice trembled. "Back off."

Neither man listened to Max. The one that had stumbled backward was now tugging on Jack, trying to pull him off his fellow worker.

"Freeze or I'll shoot," Max shouted, again.

This time, he caught both men's attention, but they did not stop fighting with Jack. Jack was so pumped, he managed to force the first worker backward again, but this time the worker stumbled and hit his head on a bench. The second one was still fighting with Jack over the handgun. Max ran up to the fallen worker who was holding his head as he began to stand. But Max stopped him when the man noticed Max pointing the rifle at point blank range. He froze.

"Put the gun on the floor and push it toward me," Max said while Jack and the other worker threw fists at each other.

The man did as Max instructed. Max picked up the gun and having previously looked at Jack's alien weapon, he dialed it down to stun and shot the man. He fell limp to the floor.

When Jack saw what Max had accomplished, he shoved the worker so hard he made enough space for Max to fire the alien beam, and he did. The man dropped.

"Shit, Max," Jack said, rubbing his jaw. "You're getting good at this."

Max was trembling so uncontrollably that he had to sit down on a bench. Jack lowered the top of his coveralls enough to stuff the nonworking alien handgun into his back waistband. He took the hip holsters from both men, tossing one toward Max. Then he took their ID tags. "Here put this on."

Max looked at the picture. "It doesn't look anything like me."

"No one's going to get close enough to see it," Jack said, clipping his ID to the breast pocket of his green coveralls. "We have to do something with them because I don't know how long they'll be out."

"Take their walkie-talkies, too," Max said, clipping on the ID tag.

"Walkie-talkies?" Jack laughed. "Are you from World War Two?"

"That's what they are, a handheld transceiver," Max said. "It's rather ironic that the aliens are light years ahead of us in technology, but this platform, or base on Mars, seems to have been around long before our time."

Jack attached a walkie-talkie to his belt and handed one to Max. "Put this on and let's grab us one of those golf carts and see if we can find the others."

Max tried to stand, but his legs were so wobbly he collapsed to the floor. "Jack, I need a little help."

Jack turned around and saw Max on the floor like a senior citizen who fell out of bed. "What the frickin' hell, Max. You can't walk now?"

"I don't do so well under stress," Max said. "I'll be better when I sit on one of those carts."

Jack lifted Max to a standing position. "Am I going to have to carry you?"

"I'll be okay in a minute," Max said.

Jack supported Max as they left the locker room and walked into the corridor. The workers were still occupied with unloading the spaceship as they walked up to one of the white motorized carts. They got in and Jack turned the ignition of the quiet vehicle. "Keep your eyes open for them and the dogs."

Jack pushed the pedal and drove slowly ahead, around the circumference toward the next spoke in the wheel. To the right was a wall of glass, showing the land of the dinosaurs. It kept their attention as they came up to the next corridor, leading toward the center of the complex. Jack turned and drove slowly down the hallway as they looked for anything that showed signs of the others.

When they came up to the center of the platform, the transporter glowed blue on the other side of the hub. Jack turned right, heading toward the next corridor. When he turned the corner to go down it, a worker was walking toward them.

"Shit," Max said, under his breath.

"Keep quiet," Jack said. He was going to drive past the man, but he held out his hand for them to stop. Jack did as the man wanted.

"Where are you headed?" the worker asked, looking back and forth between them both.

"We're going to check on the prisoners," Jack said, making little eye contact.

"Which prisoners?" he asked.

"The filthy human women and the kids," Jack answered, trying to speak how he imagined the workers would speak.

The worker smiled. "Oh, them. Randy's taken care of them; you won't need to concern yourself."

What did he mean by taken care of them? "Randy sent us to check on them," Jack said. "They're conniving and he wanted to make sure they were still imprisoned."

The man studied them some more. "I haven't seen you two before. What squad do you belong to?"

"We're new here," Jack said. "Haven't even had a chance to get the vaccine."

"I can fix that," the man said, looking suspiciously at them. "But what squad were you assigned to?"

"We're Patrol 24," Max said, sounding official. "We're following Randy's orders. Where are the infidels?"

Jack stared at the man's face; he was ready to reach for the gun holstered at his side. He could tell the worker was trying to decide whether to believe them or not.

"Randy gets pissed off if anyone doesn't do what he says," Jack said. "I don't think you want to be on his bad side." Jack paused. "What's your name and number?"

The man sighed and then pointed down the corridor. "They're down there."

Jack nodded and drove away, hoping the worker was not going to shoot them in the back. He looked over at Max. "How'd you know to say Patrol 24?"

"It's on the name badge," Max said, looking down at the identification. "My name's Todd."

Jack smiled. "I knew I kept you around for a reason . . . Todd."

"There's a jail cell," Max said, pointing ahead.

Jack slowed the cart and drove to the front of the bars. "I'll be damned."

"Jack, is that you?" Sarah said, hesitating to leave the others at the back of the cell.

"Yep," he said, stepping off the cart. "How do we get you out of here?"

"They used something like a key fob," Clare said, giving Dawn a hug.

Jack and Max reached into the pockets of their coveralls, feeling for a device that would open the door.

"I think I have it," Jack said, examining the round device he pulled from an inner pocket. "But I don't know how to use it."

"Let me see it," Max said, taking the fob from Jack's hand. He pointed it toward the door panel and pressed a button. The door clicked.

"It worked," Clare said, pushing the door open just as the building shook and an alarm sounded.

"Not again," Jack said, looking up at the ceiling, half expecting it to collapse on them. "We have to get back to the transporter."

They were about to run toward the transporter when the hub filled with workers.

"Put your hands up and pretend like we're taking you someplace," Jack said, pointing the alien handgun at them.

"We can't go to the transporter," Max said. "There are too many workers around it."

"Hopefully, it's another false alarm and they go away," Jack said.

"That one looks like Randy," Sarah said, watching the workers run around the core.

"That's not good," Jack said, looking at Randy. "We'll have to go someplace else until the transporter is clear."

"I don't want to go back in the cell," Clare said.

Then Jack noticed Randy looking in their direction and a worker pointing toward them. "I think we're going back to dinosaur land. But first, let's see how far we can ride this ruse. Start walking the opposite direction, like I'm taking you to the corral."

"Randy and that other guy are following us," Max said, as they pointed their guns at the others walking in front of the cart with their hands raised.

"Just act like we have things under control," Jack said. "But if Randy gets close, he'll know it's us."

The two women and three kids continued walking in front of the cart like prisoners being transported.

"Slow up," Randy shouted from behind them.

"Oh shit," Jack said. "Be ready to run."

"Stop," Randy said, getting closer.

Jack kept facing forward so Randy could not see his face as he kept driving. "We're taking them to the pen, on orders."

"Stop the cart," Randy said, his voice angry.

Jack stopped the cart and the others stopped walking. His heart was pounding. "We have orders to take them to the pen immediately."

"Whose orders?" Randy asked.

Jack heard Randy's voice a few short feet behind him. "Rausuca gave orders for them to go to the pen."

There was a moment of silence, and then Randy said, "Turn around."

"We need to follow orders," Jack said.

Randy's steps were now directly behind the cart. "Turn around."

Jack's palms were sweaty as he began turning around. Was there a chance Randy would not recognize him?

Slowly Jack's face was fully visible to Randy. Hideous Randy. He apparently had begun taking injections again. He saw Randy's eyes narrow. Then Jack pulled his gun just as Randy pulled his.

"Well, well, well," Randy said, once more amused. "If it isn't Jack. I was wanting to see you again."

Jack looked at Randy's wrist. The prisoner bracelet was still wrapped around it. "Hey, no hard feelings. We just want to get back to Earth."

"No hard feelings?" Randy said, in disbelief. "I want to go back to Earth, too, but you seemed to have made that impossible."

"Can't the aliens take that bracelet off?" Jack asked, staying focused on Randy's bulbous eyes.

"They haven't yet," Randy said, shaking his wrist.

Jack wanted to look over at Max and see if he had his gun pulled, or if he was just sitting there like a scared little girl. However, he did not want to take his eyes off Randy. Besides, he figured he already knew the answer to that. "There's no good reason to go back to Earth. The aliens are changing the environment and there's moss—an animal moss—that has grown over everything; even the compound. There is no one at the compound, it's destroyed."

Randy thought a moment and then looked at Clare and Sarah. "Then why do you want to go back?"

Jack did not want to tell Randy that they were refueling Pegasus and heading for the deep space craft, Infinity One. "It's better than being here with people like you pointing guns at us."

Randy snorted. "Since you want to get to the pen so badly, we'll take you there."

They were still in a standoff, each pointing their gun at the other. Jack glanced at Max, who was sitting with hands raised in surrender to Randy's cohort. What the frickin' hell. Jack watched other workers run up to them. They were outnumbered in weapons. "Randy, just let us go back through the transporter and you'll never see us again."

"Lower you weapon, Jack," Randy said. "You don't have a chance. I'd just as soon shoot your ass, but the bioship could use a living meal."

Shit, the bioship. Jack had forgotten about the stomach. He ran the options through his mind. He could obey Randy, causing all of them to be put in the corral with other creatures and eventually be fed to the bioship or be traded to other space travelers. He could shoot Randy, but then he would be killed, and so would the others. Or . . . he could not think of another option. Going to the pen would at least buy them time; time to figure out what to do. Jack lowered his weapon. "You win, Randy."

"You're not as dumb as you look, Jack," Randy said, snickering. "Take them to the pen."

The other workers took Jack and Max's guns and walkie-talkies before pulling them off the golf cart. They directed everyone to start walking toward an exit.

"Put your hands up," one of the workers shouted.

Jack turned around to see Randy walking back to the center of the hub while two workers ordered them to walk faster toward the door to the outside. He was getting tired of gaining weapons, only to have them taken away. He looked at Sarah walking ahead of him and the purse around her neck. He wondered if she still had the wand, but he doubted it when he noticed that Georgie did not even have his sword. If only he could count on Max to have his back, he would try to take one of the workers guns. But when he looked at Max, wobbling like he was going to fall over, he knew the boys would be better at assisting him than Max.

"Halt," said one of the workers from behind as they approached the exit door leading to the corral. There was a short static hiss from the walkie-talkie. "We're bringing out seven humans for the pen."

"Seven humans?" said the guy on the other end of the radio. "We'll get a bonus for adding humans to the pen. Bring them on through."

"Go through the door," the worker demanded.

Sarah stepped through first, followed by the others. Everyone, except Jack and Max, who still had their mini respirators on, became short of breath.

Jack wanted to give Sarah his respirator, but he thought that the guard would take it away. He was surprised their respirators, ID badges, hardhats, and holsters were not already taken. He assumed that the workers were so used to looking at other workers all day that it did not cross their minds to take the items away. Jack noticed the man at the control pedestal in front of the corral was frowning as they passed.

"You're caging two of us? What did they do?" the worker at the pedestal asked.

"They're not one of us," the worker said. "Keep walking toward the pen."

When they reached the pen, they stopped. A bonfire was burning in the center of the corral while the caged creatures huddled in groups like ladybugs.

"Lower the fence," the worker said. "Get inside, now."

They walked inside, turned around, and lowered their arms as the fence and its light barrier was raised.

Jack saw the workers laughing as they walked back toward the platform. The spaceship was still resting on top of the platform and black boxes were being transported from the ship to a holding area not far from the corral. He looked around inside the pen, hoping he did not see the pig-faced humans and hairy, horned goat people inside with them. To his dismay, he saw one of each, both staring at him and the others. He walked up to Sarah and whispered. "Don't look, but the pig face and goat are still in here."

Sarah sighed. "You've got to be kidding."

"Jibber, Miss Foo," Georgie said, kneeling down as the two dogs ran up to him and Willis.

While the three kids hugged the dogs, Max walked up to Jack. "I don't know if you've noticed, but those two characters over there are looking at us and I think they're talking about us."

Jack nodded. "Yeah, and brace yourself because they're going to be picking a fight with us pretty soon."

"Oh my God, Jack," Sarah said, stepping close to him. "They're walking over here."

TWENTY-TWO

The professor shined his flashlight around the space capsule and the tanker as Ray shut down the refueling pump and disconnected the hose from Pegasus. Now that the pump motors had stopped and it was quiet, the sound of chewing, of squirming, of hungry terraforming moss made him uneasy. "I think we should wait inside Pegasus for the others to return."

"I agree," Ray said, checking the gauges once more. "Go get the others from the RV; I'll be inside getting Pegasus ready for takeoff."

"Just don't leave without us," the professor said, lighting the path to the motorhome.

Ray laughed as he climbed up to the entry hatch.

The professor made his way to the motorhome and stepped inside. "We're going to wait inside Pegasus for Jack and the others to get back." He looked at the piles of food packed in the back half of the motorhome. "I'd like to take some of that with us, but I think it might cause a weight problem."

He walked his hefty body up to the pile of food and stuffed a crushed granola bar into his pocket. Then he picked up a container of oatmeal, a can of cocoa, and a jar of peanut butter. "No-bake chocolate peanut butter oatmeal cookies can be made with these."

"I thought you just said we can't take food," Father said, watching the professor go through the items gathered from the grocery store.

"The granola bar has little weight," the professor said, as he tossed the cookie ingredients back onto the pile. Then he turned to Tony. "How's your allergy?"

"I can see a little better," Tony said, wiping tears from his eyes as he sat up. "We'd better get moving."

The professor, Father, and Tony walked out of the motorhome and closed the door. Father guided Tony down the narrow path while the professor lit the way with his flashlight until they reached Pegasus.

"I'll climb up first," Father said, reaching for a ladder rung. "Professor, if you can help me get Tony inside . . . we'll be set."

The sound of a building collapsing inside the compound made the professor jump. "Hurry up," he said, shoving Tony up the ladder. "Those mossy animals are devouring everything."

When it was the professor's turn to climb inside, Father had to ask Ray to help. Ray reached through the opening and grabbed the professor's arm. "Put your pistol in your holster so you can climb better," Rays said, grunting as he continued pulling.

"Something has my damned shoe," the professor said, kicking his foot.

"Shit," Ray said. "Don't bring that stuff in here. Hold on, I'll be right back."

"What are you doing?" the professor asked, expelling gas from the effort of trying not to fall backward into the creeping vines.

Ray went to a cabinet and pulled out a sharp instrument. He climbed through the hatch, next to the professor, and reached down so that he was able to cut the veins. "Hurry, get inside."

When the professor made it through the opening, he fell to his knees. Then he looked at his feet and was relieved to see no vines.

Ray closed the hatch and they stood silent, listening. All they heard was the faint hum of Pegasus sitting idle. "No one goes outside without my permission."

"No problem," the professor said, standing and walking to the first chair on the lower tier of seats.

"When we take off, I want you in the center seat," Ray said, climbing into the captain's seat. "It's a weight thing."

Tony laughed.

"I'll move over now," the professor said, still breathing heavy from the climb. Then he looked around the interior. "There's not going to be enough seats for all of us."

"We'll do what we can," Ray said. "We're not going into outer space; we're just going to fly in the lower atmosphere, over Lake Michigan, to Marinette, Wisconsin. We should be okay."

The professor leaned back in the chair. "How much time do they have before we have to go?"

Ray shrugged. "I have everything on minimal support. As long as the vines don't find a crevice or way to enter the capsule, we can hold out a while."

No one spoke anymore, not even to mention thirst, hunger, or the urge to urinate. Instead, they took turns looking out portholes and sleeping in seats. Occasionally Ray would shine Pegasus's spotlight toward the compound, looking for movement. Other than an occasional building collapse or tree toppling, there was no movement. No further questions were asked about how long they could wait before Pegasus's reserves were used up and they were stranded. They would trust Ray's judgment as they waited for the others to return.

TWENTY-THREE

"Do you have that wand?" Jack asked Sarah.

Sarah shook her head. "No, they took it."

Jack raised his eyebrows and crossed his arms. "Do that Luke Skywalker stuff and summon it here."

Sarah let out an exasperated breath. "I don't think I can do that."

"It worked last time," Jack said. He shrugged as he coaxed her into trying.

"Last time?" Sarah said, shaking her head. "It didn't just fly into my hand, you know. Besides, I'm sure it's locked inside the base."

Jack gave her a stern look. "Humor me."

Sarah sighed and began concentrating on the wand, willing it to come to her, just as the man with the pig face and the hairy, horned person walked around the bonfire and stood several feet from them.

"Well, well, well," the pig-faced man said. He crossed his arms and snorted. "If it isn't the same infidels who defiled our presence before."

"I thought you were dead," Jack said, sneering.

The fire's light reflected on the hairy man's black eyes and curved horns. "We were only incapacitated for a while. I thought they fed you and your whoring kind to the ship."

Sarah could not concentrate with the creatures taunting them. She turned to Jack. "Don't let them provoke you. It's not worth it. Besides, Ray isn't here to help you."

The pig face and goat man laughed. They laughed so hard they doubled over.

Spit flew from the pig man's snout as he spoke. "It'll be easy rendering you unconscious, Jack, when all you have are women, kids, and dogs to help you."

Clare walked next to Sarah and whispered, "Keep concentrating on the wand, I'll handle this." She walked to Jack's side. "Why don't you . . . things, go mind your own business. We don't want to be here anymore than you do."

Neither creature acknowledged Clare, acting as though what she said meant nothing. Instead, they kept leering at Jack.

The goat man brushed the bristly hair back on his head and licked his lips with a long red tongue. "Humans are slop, are to be stepped on like a bug, and destroyed. The law of Zeus is the true religion. So when we've done away with you, Jack, we'll have our way with the women."

The pig face laughed.

Clare reached for Jack's tense arm. "Jack, don't let them get to you. It's only words."

"Are you going to let a woman tell you what to do?" the pigman said, moving toward them. "She's nothing more than a . . ."

Before the pig man could finish his sentence, Jack jabbed the pig's face so hard, his head turned to the side but was quickly righted.

"You humans are so weak," the pig grunted. Then a sneer formed on his snout, revealing yellow, decaying teeth.

Jack glanced over at Max who was standing next to Sarah; looking like he was going to faint at any moment. Then he looked at Clare as he kept his fighting stance. "I hope you know kung fu shit."

"Tops in my class for judo," she said placing her hands out from her chest and bringing her right foot forward.

"You're having a woman fight your battles, Jack?" the pigman snorted.

Jack's adrenaline was pumping. "Why does everyone hate me here?"

"We love ya, Jack," Clare said, winking an eye.

The creatures approached and the fight was on.

While Jack punched the pig man once again, Clare threw down the goat man, pitting his force against him. Soon the kids were doing what they could by throwing red Martian dirt into the creatures' faces. Even the dogs got into the action; Jibber nipped at the pig and goat's sensitive groin areas, while little Miss Foo barked as if she would tear them apart if they dared to go near her.

Max pushed wayward fighters away from Sarah as she stood still with her eyes closed. Fortunately, the creatures tended to avoid them, probably because of Max's green worker coveralls, he thought.

Sarah kept concentrating even though it was difficult with the calamity breaking out around her. Nonetheless, it felt like it was working, but she could not tell for sure.

But she did know that it felt like there was a connection between her and the wand. So much so, she was becoming oblivious to the chaos inside the corral.

TWENTY-FOUR

"What's that sound?" a worker said, stopping in the corridor of the platform just outside the property room.

"Let's check it out," the second worker said, taking his handgun from its holster. He opened the door and turned on the light. "There's nothing in here but confiscated items."

They looked in the direction of the stacked cubes, the size of a hat box. The one on the top rattled as if something inside was banging against the box's walls, trying to get out.

"An animal?" the first worker said, acting a little spooked.

"No way," the second said, frowning. "We don't keep them in here. You know that."

"Maybe one got caught in a box while we were tagging the contents," the first said, staring at the rattling container. "You know how there's weird prehistoric shit inside this volcano."

They walked closer to it as the banging turned to tapping. They looked at each other.

"Is it Morse code?" the second said, listening.

"What's it saying?" the first said, keeping his gun pointed at the sound.

"Quiet," the second said, moving closer. After moments of concentration, he said, "It sounds like three dots, three dashes, and three dots. I think it's tapping an SOS message."

"Maybe we should open it?" the first said, walking up to it. "it might be important."

The second worker stepped back while the first keyed in a code on the box. The tapping stopped as the worker lifted the lid and looked inside. "It's an alien staff. I wonder . . ."

Before the worker could close and lock the lid, the wand rose up and shot a beam of gold light at both workers; dropping them to the floor. It flew out of the room, down the corridor, and through the exit until it settled on Sarah's open palm.

Sarah opened her eyes as people were running and falling around her; everyone in the corral was now engaged in fighting. She turned and faced the pig, and when she had a clear shot, she zapped him and then the goat. They both fell unconscious to the ground.

"Everyone, stop fighting, or I'm going to knock you out, too," she shouted.

Creatures were yelling and running, not paying attention to Sarah or even noticing the pig and goat sprawled on the rust colored gravel.

Jack brought his aching fingers to his bloody mouth and whistled. It was so loud it sounded like he was a referring making a call. "Stop fighting or the guards are going to electrocute all of us."

He had everyone's attention. They all calmed down, just as a couple workers ran out of the platform, one to the pedestal and the other to the corral.

"What was going on here?" he shouted at them, like a commander ready to make everyone do an impossible number of pushups. Then blinding floodlights came on, causing some creatures to turn away.

"It's fine," Jack said, bending over with his hands on his thighs so that he could catch his breath. "Just a little squabble."

"What happened to them?" the guard said, pointing his gun toward the pig and goat.

Jack turned and looked at the unconscious beasts. "Oh, them. They're fine, just playing a little too rough. They ended up knocking each other out."

"Why is your face all bloody?" the guard asked.

"We were just playing around," Jack said. He wiped the blood from his mouth with the side of his hand.

The guard frowned. "One more outburst and I'll make the fence shock you all at maximum. Understand?"

They all nodded.

The floodlights went out as the guards walked back inside the platform.

Sarah slipped the wand into her purse and went up to Clare. "Are you okay?"

"Yeah, I'm all right," Clare said, rubbing her arms. She looked at Jack and his bloody cuts. "Jack took the brunt of it."

"I'm beaten to hell," Jack said, testing his jaw. "That pig has muscles the size of . . . well, a pig, and that goat has fingernails as hard as hoofs." He turned to Clare, who was limping like an old woman. "You kick ass, Clare."

"Don't get me involved in any more of your fights, Jack," Clare said, placing a hand on her hip.

As the crackling bonfire died down, whimpers from the delicate vine people and other fragile ones in the pen floated through the air. It was not that they were hurt, but rather, frightened by the events that had just occurred.

"I got the wand," Sarah whispered.

"How?" Clare said.

"I willed it here," Sarah said.

"You're getting better with that thing," Clare said, stretching to the side.

"Get us out of here, then," Jack said, taking another look at the troublemakers still on the ground.

Sarah looked at the blue lights on top of the poles of the fence surrounding the corral. "If I lower the fence, the alarms will probably sound and we'll have to deal with the guards coming back out here."

Jack looked at the lit poles and then back to Sarah. "What did you have in mind?"

"Nothing, really." Sarah shrugged.

Jack looked up at the transparent blue dome surrounding the Martian base. He touched the back of his aching neck and rubbed it. "There's no barrier above us. Maybe you could shoot a beam to a faraway spot on the far side of the dome and the guards will think a dinosaur is trying to break in. While that alarm is sounding and the guards are running that direction, you can lower this fence and we'll run inside the base and into the transporter."

"I guess," Sarah said. "I'll probably have to shoot people along the way because I don't think they're all going to run out and go the opposite direction as us."

"That's fine with me," Jack said. "When you knock them out with that wand I'll be able to grab their handguns."

"That might work," Clare said. "But we should do it soon before the sun rises and they lower the dome and those crazy creatures wake up."

Sarah looked at the kids. "Okay, you guys; when the fence goes down, we're running. Make sure someone's carrying Miss Foo and that Jibber is following us."

Georgie picked up the little teacup poodle. "I'm ready."

"Make sure you don't accidentally hit the fence when you're shooting over it," Jack said, spitting blood onto the ground.

Sarah nodded and extended her arm, aiming the wand for a spot on the dome as far away from them as she could. She concentrated and beam shot from the wand to the curved dome wall on the far side of the ship. The second the beam hit the interior of the dome, an alarm sounded. Workers and guards ran out of the base with weapons drawn, heading for the injured dome.

"I think you punctured a hole through it," Jack said, watching the workers only glance their way as they ran. "Now, lower the fence."

Sarah aimed at the fence. "Stand back," she said, as the wand disabled the barrier.

"Let's go," Jack said, leading the way through the perimeter toward the platform door.

The blue glow from the dome throbbed with the warning sirens, emitting enough light to see through the darkness. When they reached the door of the platform, Jack looked through the transparent shield covering the entrance; no one was in view. He motioned for Sarah to place her hand over the lock symbols to open the door. The shield flickered but did not drop. She put her hand up to it and was able to push through.

"It's unlocked," she said, walking through the door.

Everyone followed her through the entrance and down the corridor toward the center hub of the base, and the transporter. Jack motioned for everyone to stop while he looked around the corner to see if anyone was coming their way.

Jack turned to the others and whispered, "There are people in the control room, and they'll probably see us when we run for the transporter."

"Let's just go for it, Jack," Clare said.

"Okay," Jack said, wiping sweat from his brow. "Clare, you lead the kids and Max to the transporter, and Sarah and I will bring up the rear." He turned to Sarah. "Be ready to shoot if . . . I mean when they see us, because they will."

Jack held up three fingers and whispered. "One, two, three."

On three, Clare ran across the open center hub to the transporter's blue glow; she disappeared inside. Dawn, Georgie, Willis, the dogs, along with Max, who was tripping over Jibber as they ran single file.

"They see us," Jack said, looking toward the workers beginning to run out of the control room. "Shoot 'em."

Sarah pointed the wand at the guards who were leaving the glassed-in cage of the operations area as an alarm sounded and lights flashed. The wand's beam had no effect on the guards inside the protected room. But any that were leaving it to fire at them ended up incapacitated, as the wand's beam hit them like a Mack

Truck, forcing them backward. They slid across the floor like rag dolls tossed by a toddler having a tantrum.

"I'm getting a gun," Jack said, running up to one of the unconscious guards. He pulled it out of its holster and fired at the next guard coming out of the control room.

As Jack ran for the transporter, he shouted, "Get in it, now."

TWENTY-FIVE

The professor's snoring was interrupted when an alarm sounded inside the Pegasus space capsule.

"Shit," Ray said, studying the control panel.

"What's that sound?" Tony asked. His allergy had improved enough for him to see the pulsating red lights.

Ray did not answer while he pressed buttons on the screens. "Something is trying to breach the ship."

"It's probably the vines," the professor said, now awake. "They're either trying to find a way inside or are covering us like they did the buildings in the compound."

Tony rubbed his eyes and looked toward a porthole. "I'm able to see a little better, but are my eyes playing tricks on me?"

Ray looked toward a window. "Oh shit, those things are wrapping around Pegasus."

"Can they trap us here?" Tony asked, getting out of his seat and walking toward a window.

"Pegasus will pack quite a punch when we take off," Ray said. "We'll probably rip them to threads but if they are intelligent, like the professor thinks, they're probably trying to find a way inside the craft."

"That is a likely scenario," the professor said, walking to another porthole. Other than a faint pink glow from the atmospheric haze, it was dark outside. However, there was enough light inside Pegasus to show suction cups, tendrils, and what appeared to be a mouth on one of the nodules of the vine's red veins. "I know the capsule is designed for space flight and is airtight, but I wouldn't put it past these things to be intelligent enough to figure out a way inside or at least begin digesting us."

"Have they digested metal before?" Tony asked, turning to look at the professor who was examining the creatures.

Father stood up and ran a finger between his neck and clerical collar. "I'd say that if they can tear down the buildings in the compound, then they can weaken metal."

"It would take a lot to break through the carbon composite exterior of Pegasus," Ray said. "The ship is designed to withstand the heat of reentry. But if the vines have a substance, an alien chemical that we aren't aware of, then who knows."

"How much time do we have before we need to liftoff?" the professor asked, turning to look at Ray.

Ray silenced the alarm while red lights flashed silently in the cabin. "I don't know for sure. Right now, there is no breach, but once they breach the hull, we should leave. I'll keep watching it."

"Maybe we can go outside and tear them off the capsule," Tony said, blowing his nose on a snot-soaked tissue. "Now that I can see better, I'll do it."

"They'll eat you alive," the professor said. "I think it is best we kept everything tight and sealed until the others get back . . . hopefully soon."

Tony turned back to the circular window and studied the vines of the animal clinging to the glass. He jumped back when an eye opened on a nodule of a stem. "That damned thing is more animal than plant; it just looked at me with an eye."

The professor walked over to where Tony was pointing. "I'll be damned."

The alarm began sounding again.

"I thought you silenced that," Tony said. He walked away from the window, deciding he had seen enough.

"There are several areas that are close to being breached," Ray said, wiping perspiration from his forehead. "I hate to say it, but if the others aren't back in the next few minutes, we'll have to leave." He pulled the safety belt over his body and buckled it. "Strap in."

TWENTY-SIX

Sarah disappeared inside the beam with Jack right behind her. Jack had just stepped out of the transporter in the church's sacristy when the shaft of light disappeared.

Jack looked at the non-existent transport beam and then up at the collapsing ceiling. "I don't know if it's good or bad, but it appears that the guards have no interest in following us through the transporter."

"They've made it so we can't go back," Sarah said, looking at the dark corner where the blue light once glowed.

"I'm not complaining," Jack said, walking through the sacristy door, past empty pews, to the main entrance.

"Jack, cut us a path out of here," Clare said, motioning for the kids to get close to Jack.

Jack dialed the alien handgun to destroy the plants without burning up everything the ray beam came into contact with.

"The door won't open all the way," Willis said, helping Jack tug on the broken and crushed wood.

Jack yanked on the door as plants squirmed around the opening. "Stand back," he said as he shot at the vines that were attempting to wiggle across the church floor.

The ceiling of the church was caving in as chewing and gnawing filled their ears. Jack finally worked a space large enough for them to fit through. He shot a beam through the opening, killing the creepy vines. He squeezed out the opening and stopped as he looked around the prepper compound. He was surprised to see it nearly flattened and covered by the creeping creatures.

"Shit, this is not good. I hope they haven't left without us," Jack said, as the others climbed through the opening.

He cut a path toward the gate. They were walking until they heard Pegasus's engines power up like a rocket was getting ready to launch.

"That's Pegasus," Jack said, breaking into a run. "They're leaving without us."

The gang ran so fast their quick feet could have burned their own path through the terraforming mess. Jack waved his hands, as did everyone else, as they shouted and jumped, trying to get Ray's attention. Jack ran to the cab of the semi-truck and laid on the air horn. It was so loud it sounded like a train was barreling through The Community. He sounded it again, hoping the others could hear it from inside the capsule.

Then Pegasus powered down and the hatch opened. Ray poked out his head. "Hurry, get inside."

Jack killed the terraforming creatures from around the base of Pegasus as everyone climbed inside. Jack was last in and closed the hatch while Ray re-ignited the rockets.

"There are not enough seats for everyone," Sarah said, looking around.

"We're not going into space," Ray said, concentrating on the panel. "Some of you can just hold onto the cargo straps."

"The kids and I can do that," Jack said, securing them in the cargo hold. "Just get us out of here."

Max sat next to Ray, watching the screen while the kids held Jibber and Miss Foo securely. It was a madhouse inside as alarms sounded and the rockets reignited.

"Hold on," Ray said, gripping the control stick as if he were playing a video game.

The capsule rumbled and roared as it lifted off Earth and away from the terraforming creatures. Fiery lights flared outside the portholes, turning night into a blazing furnace. Pegasus accelerated, producing a g-force that pressed them into the craft. It was loud and they were moving fast.

Jack looked at Ray and he could tell he was stressed, by the way his face was contorted. He frantically looked at the control monitors as he gave instructions to Max to help in the navigation to Infinity One in Wisconsin. It felt like they were going to blow up like a bomb, but as they reached a higher altitude things eased up, but not much. Jack looked at Sarah, gripping the strap across her body. He was surprised when she turned her head and looked at him. He smiled and she smiled back.

"It won't take long to get to the ISP headquarters and our next ride," Ray shouted above the roar. "We're doing fine; I already had the flight path programmed in. Just hang tight."

Hang tight? Jack smiled. He was hanging tight all right, tight to the cargo straps like a crate of Wisconsin cheese. "I'm kissing the ground when we land," he shouted back.

"One of those critters will kiss you back and take a bite of your lip," Tony said over the roar. "We saw them close-up while waiting for you guys."

"I'm hoping Wisconsin isn't infested," Jack shouted.

"I think the whole planet is covered with that shit," Max shouted as he looked over his shoulder at Jack and the kids. "But you can kiss the ground if you want, Jack."

The flight was intense; it was as if they were riding a nuclear warhead to enemy soil.

Sarah kept running through her mind all the things that they were leaving behind. Her house and all her family photos. The kids baby clothes and scrapbooks. Her relatives and friends, most of which she assumed had been affected by the alien spores. She imagined her home swallowed up by the carpet of moss and vines, and the kids' school projects that were now pointless. There were other projects to work on now, mostly survival. She looked toward the kids, safe next to Jack, and then at a porthole. She assumed they were now over Lake Michigan, but there was no getting out of her chair to look out and see if she could see anything.

It was not long and they felt the fall of the craft as the thrusters kicked in and Pegasus began descending, falling back to Earth.

"Hang on," Ray shouted. "We'll be landing soon."

Sarah remembered hearing that the most dangerous parts of flight were the takeoff and the landing. They survived the takeoff, now Ray had to set the craft gently onto the ground, close to Infinity One. She could not help but wonder what they would find if Ray did manage to land safely. Would they be where they needed to be, or would they be surrounded by the piranha vines, and have no vehicles to drive in which to escape. She would know the answer soon enough.

The craft roared and trembled as it decelerated and landed with a gentle thud on the ground.

"We've landed!" Ray said, as Pegasus hissed and popped.

Everyone cheered and gave Ray a round of applause. No one stood; they were waiting for Ray to give the okay. Outside the portholes, there was a faint pink glow from the rising sun. They could not tell what it looked like outside until they stood and looked out the small exterior windows.

Ray unstrapped and smiled. "It's okay to move around. When Pegasus cools, we can go outside."

The first place everyone went was to the portholes. Laughter and smiles turned to moans and drooped heads.

"Ray, look at this," Jack said, peering out a porthole next to Sarah.

Ray stood and walked to look outside.

"Where are we?" Jack asked. "I don't see that space facility or that giant spaceship you were talking about. Are you sure we landed in the right place?"

Ray frowned as he looked out at the same moss-covered landscape. "I think those lumps over there is the facility. It must have been swallowed by those damned critters."

"Does that mean the Infinity One is gone, too?" Sarah asked, saddened by the site. It was like they ended up in a place no better than the one they had just left.

Ray smiled. "Yep, we're in the right place, Infinity One is fine."

"How do you know?" Jack asked, frowning.

"Do you see that clearing over there?" Ray pointed toward a football field sized flat area where the moss was avoiding. "That's where Infinity One is."

"Where?" Jack asked. "I don't see it, or any spaceship."

"To protect the ship from being spotted by satellites, we were able to develop an invisible hanger," Ray said, grinning. "In fact, the Infinity One is able to use the same cloaking device. And since there is no moss where the hanger is, means it wasn't able to get inside the highly secured facility."

"You're a genius, Ray," Jack said, slapping him on the back. "I guess fighting that pig face and hairy goat man to rescue your ass was worth it."

Ray strutted back to the captain's seat and smiled. "And you remember that."

While they waited for Pegasus to cool, Jack and Max explained why they were dressed like the workers on Mars and how they kicked the butts of the pig and goat once more. Of course, Clare pointed out that she did a lot of ass-kickings, too.

When Pegasus exterior temperature had dropped enough, Ray informed them that it was time to leave. He opened the hatch as steam rose from the craft. "Don't touch anything when you get out, it's still hot."

Jack used the alien handgun to clear a path toward where Ray said the hanger door was. Everyone got out and followed Ray to the invisible building. Within minutes, he had the door opened, and they stepped inside where the huge spaceship sat in the center, like a shining UFO.

When they were inside, Ray locked the hanger door. They stood there in awe, admiring the intergalactic spacecraft. On the side of the dark silver craft was the words INFINITY ONE - ISP.

"The Intercosmic Space Program sure knew what they were doing when they made this magnificent vessel," the professor said, walking as if he was fifty pounds lighter.

"See what I mean when I say the government is good at hiding things," Tony said, clenching his jaw.

"This isn't a government project," Ray said, walking up to the side of the craft. "It's designed and made by a private enterprise with no government funding."

"Where's the funding from?" Max asked, lifting an eyebrow.

Ray did not answer.

"It looks like Jupiter 2 on Lost in Space," Sarah said, standing between Ray and Jack.

Ray nodded in agreement and walked up to it. He held out his hand and within seconds a door opened on the side of the craft and a platform lowered. "Come on, let's get inside."

They stood there for a moment, in shock. Not believing how Ray just opened the door by simply holding out his hand.

The professor walked as quickly as his fat legs would carry him toward the ramp. "How'd you do that?"

Ray got to the top of the platform and looked back at the others, now walking up behind him. "It's a transplant."

For the first time since meeting Ray, Sarah felt like there was more to him than being an ordinary astronaut. She walked next to Jack, bringing up the rear, and whispered, "I just got an uneasy feeling about Ray."

Jack looked at her. "Yeah, me too. But we have to tag along for the ride."

When everyone was inside and through the airlock, the doors closed. Ray was on the flight deck looking at control panels before taking a seat in one of the three chairs secured in front of a table of monitors and transparent images, all facing the large forward window.

Sarah was in awe at the feel of the interior. The air was fresh and the lighting was soft. There was an elevator, leaving her to wonder how many levels the craft had. There was what looked like white coffins with see-through tops, probably used for long spaceflights, she thought. There was even what appeared to be a robot toward the center of the room; it was life-size and not moving, apparently waiting for a command that would bring it to life.

Tony walked up to Jack. "Look over there."

Jack and Sarah looked out the front wall of windows. In the far side of the hanger, was a parked black Cadillac.

"The black caddy?" Jack said. "What about it?"

"It belongs to the Men in Black," Tony said, crossing his arms. "I think they have something to do with Infinity One."

"Maybe it belongs to Ray," Jack said, smiling as he teased Tony.

"I'm serious," Tony said, watching Ray. "I think we need to keep an eye on him."

Ray looked back at the others. "Take a seat, we'll be taking off. There's no need to strap in, it's a pretty smooth ride."

They walked to seats lined up against the back wall. They had barely sat down when they noticed Infinity One rising through the top of the hanger.

"I can't feel it moving," Willis said, holding onto Jibber. "I like this."

Tony could not help himself; he had to ask. "Ray, whose Cadillac was that in the hanger?"

"It's mine," Ray said, as Infinity One gracefully ascended.

* * *

Thank you for reading!

Visit Connie's website at ConnieMyres.com

NO-BAKE CHOCOLATE PEANUT BUTTER OATMEAL COOKIES

Ingredients
    3 cups sugar
    2/3 cup butter
    3 tablespoons cocoa
    1/2 cup milk
    Combine and bring to a boil (about one minute).
Then add:
    2/3 cup peanut butter
    3 cups oatmeal

Directions
Remove from heat and drop by spoonful onto wax paper.

Notes
The professor mentioned these cookies in Chapter Twenty-Two.

"This is a handwritten recipe from my mom's kitchen and is probably the one she made a lot when I was a kid. It dates back to at least the 1970s."

~ Connie Myres

Read the Next Book in the Series

TRIBULATION (SEVEN SEALS REDUX, #5)

Forced off Earth because of an alien invasion, our haggard crew must find a new home. While Infinity One is designed for deep space flight, it is virtually untested as it sets out on its maiden voyage into the solar system.

Running from the aliens and plagued by disasters, the gang retreats to the moon and Proxima b. However, fate has a mind of her own when they end up back on Mars. The fifth seal opens full force when they meet up once again with ol' Randolph Watson.

A crew member turns on the others. Jack is stranded and alone. And Sarah takes on a new and unexpected role.

Follow the exhausted team and find out who must be sacrificed to appease the gods.

Get the Details at Connie's Website

https://www.ConnieMyres.com

Also by Connie Myres

STANDALONE BOOKS

Jezebel • My Name is Mr. Dibble • Ring • Haunting of Ender House • Rest Stop Terror • Solus • Who Killed Sweet Violet? • Lucifer's Island • Raven's Ridge

PACIE ROSE MYSTERIES

Slenderman • Hornet

RANCOR

Rancor: A Paranormal Psychological Thriller (Books 1 & 2) Sinister Attachments • Unrestrained

SEVEN SEALS REDUX

Seven Seals Redux: The Complete Apocalyptic Novel Series (Books 1-7)
White Horse • Red Horse • Black Horse • Pale Horse • Tribulation • Signs • Trumpets

SUSPENSE STORIES

Suspense Stories #1: Raven's Ridge, Lucifer's Island, Sinister Attachments (Suspense Stories, #1)

THREE SISTERS ODYSSEY (SERIAL)

Read Episodes As Connie Writes Them

WATCH FOR SPOOKY SHORTS

A collection of creepy short stories, A-Z.

Spooky Shorts A-G: A Collection of Creepy Short Stories

Apple Pie • Black-Eyed Kids • Creature • Dungeon • Electric • Fairy • Genie • House • Ice • Joker • Kiss • Lucid • Minion • Neighbor • Obelisk • Pattern • Quest • Rumor • Squatch • Time • Underworld • Visitor • Wolf • X-axis • Yellow • ZoZo.

* * *

Find all the books at https://www.ConnieMyres.com

About the Author

CONNIE MYRES writes books and short stories in the horror, mystery, suspense, and science fiction genres. She is an author, developer, and registered nurse. Sometime in the future—whether by choice or by arm-twisting—she will join the digital nomad movement.

Born and raised in Michigan, she has been creating stories since childhood. Children she had babysat as a teenager loved to hear her mystery stories, especially since she carefully included all the children listening into the storyline, causing suspense for everyone.

Connie's website: https://www.ConnieMyres.com

FEATHER AND FERMION PUBLISHING

Founded in 2014, Feather and Fermion Publishing proudly publishes horror, mystery, suspense, thriller, science fiction and fantasy stories. Our imprints—Oort Cloud Books and White-Knuckle Books—publish original fiction with the mission to entertain readers.

Author Connie Myres owns Feather and Fermion Publishing.

Visit Connie's Website

Visit Connie's website and find her blog, books, ARC team, movies, podcast, and where you can follow her on social media.

https://www.ConnieMyres.com